CW01513344

Threads of Awen

Awen Thornber

A collection of short stories, flash fiction and
poems drawn from inspiration.

Best Wishes

Awen Thornber

x x

Threads of Awen © Awen Thornber 2017

This is a work of fiction. Names, characters and incidents are used fictitiously.

ISBN: 978-1978141421

Editor: Jeff Gardiner
Cover Design: goonwrite.com
Formatting: Rebecca Emin

Introduction

What is Awen?

Awen is a druid word, probably originating from Wales, Cornwall and Breton, and has a literal translation of 'poetic inspiration.'

It has also been translated as being the inspirational muse for creative artists.

Inspiration can be found everywhere.

Don't just look for inspiration in landscapes, photographs, nature, but use all your senses.

How many times has a smell or scent reminded you of a holiday or person? Lily of the valley always reminds me of my Nan.

Do you listen to conversations on the train or in the supermarket? I've often found just a few words from the conversation can trigger a whole plot.

Textures conjure up memories too. The lightest touch of holding a bird on your palm or the rough brick on your skin as you scrape past a wall.

My grandson's face was a picture of disgust, when he tasted his first spoon full of baby rice.

All these everyday things are easy to dismiss, but I note them down and can then use them in poems, short stories and novels.

All of the pieces in this anthology have used my inspiration notes in some way.

I have included a description of the source used for the flash fiction pieces where the inspiration was always a photograph.

Acknowledgements

I would like to thank Anne, who has been my brainstorming friend, encouraging and nagging me for over fifteen years to keep writing even when life got in the way.

Thanks also go to Catherine for her encouragement and support and my husband Peter, daughter Gill and son Phillip for believing in me.

Last but not least for friends Paula and Carol for meeting up and chatting about writing every month. Our meetings at Costa always sparked new ideas.

To my parents Alan and Marjorie Thornber

Contents

Looking For Lucas	1
Walking in my Girlfriend's Shoes.	5
Ross	7
A Thorny Problem	8
Today is another day	13
Gran's Calling	15
Ashes to ashes	17
One Fine Place	19
For the love of Rosie.	20
Lads' night. A Sonnet	32
Train of Thought.	33
Nelson	35
War 1916	36
Plumber's Mate	41
Giving them wings.	43
The Turning of Autumn.	45
Frost Giants	47
The Princess and The Dragon.	48
I Did It My Way.	54
Flibbertigibbet	56
The Antique Emporium	58
My Husband's Eyes. A Sonnet	63
Betula and Ulmus	64
Daughter of Hades.	65
Lost In The Storm	67
Rough with smooth.	78
Defying the odds	80
A Greek Tragedy.	90
Wicked words and dastardly deeds.	91
Going Boldly on Bold Street	98
Dodgy Business	99
Bradley's Reward.	105
A Creative Culture	107
A Special Delivery.	109
Turn around Toxteth.	115
A Cloud of Doubt	116
Stanley and Eleanor	120
Lost Baby	121
When You Came Into My Life	122
About the Author	125

Looking For Lucas

I stood by the window.

The rain oozed through a gap in the wooden frame and trickled down to the sill.

A small hand crept into my left hand. It felt cold and clammy: or was it sticky? The fingers curled into my palm and around my thumb trustingly. It stayed there tucked into mine. I closed my hand over it automatically.

It seemed to me that many years had passed since I held my child's hand, although it had only been two years since the accident.

We just stood there. Very still. For a long while. Still.

For longer than I wanted – longer than I intended – I stayed silent.

I didn't want him to vanish. I didn't want to break this spell of mother and son holding hands once again.

I could have wept, but I didn't.

Instead, I whispered. I kept my voice low in an attempt to draw out this precious moment. The angels had brought him to me as I had asked them to; and here he was.

He was here beside me

I was holding my son's hand.

He was close to me once more. My boy, who could never keep still for long, who found all of life fun, until that fateful day, just stood beside me.

Still.

Wordless.

My chattering noisy son said nothing, but as I slowly looked down on his golden curly locks and pale skin, he looked up at me with eyes so filled with love that it was all I could do, not to cry out.

I spoke so softly that he could have mistaken it

for the fall of a leaf or the wisp of a breeze, but he understood.

I knew he understood.

A mother's instinct? The strong bond of a mother and son? He listened as I spoke.

'I love you, Lucas'

A slight nod. His eyes fastened on my face.

'I will always love you, Lucas.'

Again that slight nod and a barely perceptible tightening of his fingers around my thumb.

'You were just a two year old when they took you from me. Do you understand?'

He blinked. I knew he understood.

A shout pierced the moment. I looked up, Lucas looked away.

I could feel his hand slipping from mine. I couldn't show emotion. I wanted to hold this blond-haired boy of mine once more. I couldn't cuddle him, of course.

'Will you come again tomorrow?'

The space in my hand that had once been filled with his was now painfully empty.

'I would like to see you again. I will wait for you here, in this very spot. Will you come?'

My child nodded and was gone.

I had suppressed my emotion and the maternal feelings he had stirred, whilst he was standing by my side. Holding my hand. I couldn't risk sending him away forever. I had to tread carefully so as not to push him away.

I whispered again to the wind.

'I will wait for you.'

I waited again in the studio.

I waited from first light, trying not to think of the possible scenarios that would prevent him from coming.

I stood looking out of the window. The garden around the studio was overgrown. It had once been neat. Fairy ornaments had danced around the flowers and path. Around the door I had tacked fairy lights, and Lucas thought it magical.

There was a strong smell of honeysuckle. It had taken hold of the outside of the studio and run rampant, wrapping itself around the walls and roof. Entrails of it squeezed through all the gaps in the wooden walls and what was left of the roof and spilled over on to the floor.

The light trespassed through the grubby window and fell onto the toy garage I had been making for Lucas that day. It stood there covered in muck, dust and webs like some unloved, derelict, inner city petrol station.

I had been standing at the window in the studio. Lucas was with me playing on his trike. In and out of the studio.

In and out.

In and out.

There was a storm brewing. I called him in out of the rain. I saw a flash then heard a loud crack, and all of a sudden the roof caved in.

I screamed.

Den, our neighbour, came rushing over. He saw me holding on to Lucas. Holding on to my son, my dear son.

It was too late.

They pulled him away from me.

The sky was quickly becoming grey. It was going to rain. The light was fading fast, and the clouds had gathered in an angry blanket overhead.

I feared he would not come.

I waited longer than I intended, never taking my eyes off the window.

He isn't coming, I told myself. But as I stood

there his hand slipped into mine, and I squeezed it gently.

There it was again. That look of love. Those trusting eyes gazed at my face.

I smiled at him.

'I will always love you, Lucas. I will always be your mummy.'

'Love you, Mummy.'

I could have wept.

'Lucas! Lucas! There you are. What are you doing out here?'

I reached out to my Mother, but she didn't see. She walked straight through me, to sweep up Lucas into her arms.

'Mummy.'

'No, Lucas, darling. Mummy's gone. Mummy's joined the angels. I saw the tears in her eyes. 'Come with Nanny. We'll bake some cookies.'

I watched as they walked down the garden path.

Lucas turned and held up his little hand in a wave.

I waved back and blew him a kiss.

His tiny lips made a 'mwah', then he turned back to my Mother and snuggled into her neck as they went into the house.

I knew he wouldn't visit me at the studio again. The next time he sees me he will be old with children and grandchildren of his own.

I felt a presence behind me and heard the rustle of opening wings.

'Are you ready?'

'Yes.'

I was enveloped in brilliant light.

'Bye, Lucas.'

Walking in my Girlfriend's Shoes

Photograph: A couple holding hands looking down on a city. We can only see the back of them. The one on the right is wearing a short dress, the other a pair of trousers. The photo is black and white.

It was time to open the door.

When they first met they discovered a common ground. It bound them together.

Theirs was a freedom which kept them a prisoner.

Take their careers for instance.

He: a fire fighter.

She: a model.

They discussed the expectations which accompanied their roles.

"You have a heroic career and the appearance of a Greek God, but you're complaining that it attracts too many women? Is it such a hard status to live up to?"

"It's alright for you," he said, "all you have to do is look pretty and pose for the camera."

"You want to try walking in these shoes." She said.

So he did.

He liked it.

His inner gaoler locked him in the room with the black dog, then threw away the key.

"Why don't you leave me here?" he said.

"Your prison is my prison," she said.

He looked deep into her eyes, saw his reflection mirrored in there and cried.

He rested his head on her shoulder and played

5

with her long brown hair.

"I am feeling how you are feeling," she said.

"That is exactly how it is," he said.

Being caged is a lonely existence, cooped up in one room, and now the door was unlocked.

"Let's go." She turned to look at the pile of long thick brown hair, on the tiled floor by the sink.

Then smoothed her palm over the new cropped style, before she dug her hands into her trouser pockets.

In contrast he flicked his long fair hair from his shoulder, and smoothed down his dress.

They stepped out onto the sunlit road, and faced the town.

They'd found their freedom, unlocked the chains binding them to expectations.

Each walked forward and onward, heads held high, in their girlfriend's shoes.

Ross

My puppy was an orphan
We brought him home from Devon
His mummy ate rat poison
And has a place in doggy heaven.
She never saw her little pups
Which makes me sad, you see,
So I give him a mother's love
And he gives big love to me.

Border collie, Ross. 1997-2011

A Thorny Problem

I awoke with a start.

The glare from the sun was blinding. Panic rose with a lump in my throat and the feeling of a heavy weight jumping on my chest.

In an effort to discover where I was, I struggled to recall what had woken me up. I rubbed the sleep from my eyes and opened them properly. I felt as though I had been asleep for a hundred years; my eyelids were heavy and I felt sickly.

I had a distinct memory of bristles that felt like short stubby fur, brushing my face and a less certain memory of a warm draught on my cheek, that could possibly have been warm breath. It was tainted with a horrible stale smell.

A shadow fell across me. At first all I could make out against the sun's glare was a mass of twisted branches from trees or something. Then the silhouette of a large head from some sort of creature loomed over me. It had short ears and broad shoulders and I struggled to recognise the shape.

A bear maybe?

I tried to scream.

"All right, love," boomed the creature's deep voice. "Keep the noise down. Anyone would think I'm trying to murder you, not help you."

I tried to move out of the way by shuffling on my bottom, struggled to get myself into a sitting position, but I was wrapped in some sort of thick fabric bag, and I floundered like a mermaid out of water.

I started to scream again, when the sun went behind a cloud and the area around me became clear and was no longer black and white. I could see that the twisted branches were thorny brambles, and more importantly, that the bear was

8

no more than a scruffy man.

I stopped screaming and anger took the place of fear.

"Why have you brought me here?" I demanded.

"Why have I brought *you* here?"

"That's what I said." Sarcasm took the place of fear.

"I didn't bring you here, you were here already"

"I was here already?"

"That's what I said."

"Oh funny, aren't you." I looked around. "Then where am I?"

"You don't know?"

"Would I be asking if I knew?" Really this man was a fool, or was he clever and playing mind games with me.

The sun was trying to dodge the clouds. I peered at him.

"Who are you?" I asked, "And what do you want from me?"

"I'm Phil Prince, of Prince and Son builders and I don't want anything from you, except of course for you to move off my land so I can carry on digging"

"*Your* Land?"

"That's what I said"

I gave him my special withering look.

"Then what am I doing on your land?"

"You tell me."

"Would I be asking if I knew?" I gave an exasperated sigh.

"Ok," he said slowly and paused. He looked pained. He obviously found the thinking process difficult!

I took the opportunity to look at him closely. Why was I in this strange place with this unkempt man? He was wearing a filthy vest with his dirty stained pants slung low under his rounded belly, several days' growth of hair on his face, and the same amount of hair on his head. He had an earring in one ear and his tanned arms were decorated with tattoos and angry bloodied cuts.

"This is Stefan Villas. Ring any Bells?"

I shook my head. It didn't mean anything to me. He was staring at me and it unnerved me.

"This is my property. I bought it at the auctions. Got it dirt cheap with it being derelict, and as soon as you move out of your sleeping bag and go home, I'm going to turn it into apartments." He had another thought; I knew that because a fleeting look of pain crossed his face.

"Who are you?" he asked. "What's your name?"

"I'm..." But the name wouldn't come. Who was I? I must remember my name, but what on earth was it.

"Can't remember," I mumbled. I was embarrassed. I looked at my hands as though they held some clue but they were bare and empty and didn't help. Then I looked down at my body encased in this strange bag. The bag had a row of roses, small crowns and the word 'Rose' embroidered on it along the top edge. There was a label sewn into the side, one word, 'Aurora'. I shook my head.

"No, not a clue. Can't remember" Again the feeling of panic gripped me. Worse than knowing that I was in a strange place, was the not knowing who I was.

I heard the sound of chopping wood then an older man appeared through a gap in the brambles.

"Hello, son. You wake her up then?"

"Yeah, Bert, but I reckon she must have had a bang on the head. Says she can't remember who she is, where she is, or why."

Bert seemed to consider this.

10

"Is there someone we can contact for you? Someone who can come and take you home?" He paused, his face registering a thought, then continued kindly. "Reckon you must be ill and homeless. My son, Phil, here," he dug Phil in the belly, "found you lying amongst these brambles. Thought you were dead, he did. You were hardly breathing, miss; don't know how long you had been like that. We had to cut our way through the thorns to get to you. They must have grown around you, no way you could have got through them otherwise."

It didn't make any sense to me.

"I can't have been that ill if I woke up just because of the sounds your son made chopping through the brambles."

Bert chuckled and Phil laughed aloud.

"No, miss," explained Bert, "you didn't wake up on your own. Our Phil had to give you the kiss of life, several times, before your breathing got back to normal."

I looked at Phil with his filthy clothes and obvious aversion to water and soap.

"Ugh, gross!" I pulled a face.

Bert grinned. "It was like true love's kiss."

"Well, don't think it will happen again!" I aimed this at Phil. "Don't get any ideas."

"No danger, love, you're no beauty. Look at yourself. You have dirt smears on your face, no make-up, cobwebs in your hair, not to mention the other insects nesting there, and big crusts of sleep in the corner of your eyes. I reckon you could scrub up well enough, though, love." He grinned, a broad grin showing a perfect set of white teeth.

"How... how dare you!" I spluttered. I could feel the colour rise in my cheeks. I struggled a bit more in the bag and managed to wriggle free of it. I stood up, smoothed down my velvet cape and long blue

11

silk dress and faced them. Phil's face looked strangely familiar when he grinned. Had I met him before? I tried to remember, but it was so far back in my memory that I couldn't bring it to the fore.

Phil looked me up and down then winked at Bert.

"Look at the embroidered crest. We seem to be in the presence of royalty, Bert." He made an exaggerated gesture of touching his forelock and bowing.

I'd had enough, and although I hadn't a clue where I was going to, I turned to walk through the gap in the thorns.

"When you get a bit of slap on your face come back and see me and I'll show you a good time."

I flounced off with as much dignity as I could muster, sidling through the brambles, walking past their tools and stepping over an old spinning wheel.

"You needn't bother."

He laughed again and called after me.

"This was no coincidence, love. You and me; we're meant to be together. You'll be back."

"Don't hold your breath," I called back over my shoulder. "I'd have to be desperate. Who do you think you are, Prince Charming?"

Today is another day

*This poem was written because I wanted to
finish writing my novel, but my Fibromyalgia
prevented me from thinking properly.
Commonly called 'Brain Fog,' it inspired the
poem.*

Today is another day
Of fog, that blinds the mind
And suffocates the cells.
A carousel of words.
Constantly passing by
in ever turning circles
too fast to pick one out
and keep tight hold.
They dodge my grasp
like flies that buzz
annoyingly
Inside my ears,
around my head
On and on and on.
I can't catch them.
I can't grasp the words,
I can't catch the meaning
I can't make myself understood.
Then tired.

Drained.
All perseverance battered,
I give in.
I can't fight it.
Time has taught me
stress feeds the engine
that spews out
the sickly substance
that coats coherence
and becomes

my marshmallow brain.
Broken.
I had nothing to say,
of importance,
today
anyway.
Tomorrow is another day.

Gran's Calling

The inspiration for this poem was the Anthony
Gormley installation on Crosby beach, near
Liverpool, called Another Place.

My Gran was arrested again today.
Protesting above Lewis's doorway,
she'd given Dickie Lewis a hat and scarf,
then sewed boxer shorts on his lower half.
'I only want to hide his shame,' she stressed.
'It's not a crime to be properly dressed.'
It was also the day Gran was due to appear
in court, for similar offences over the year.

Despite her ripe old age of ninety-three,
the judge, who had a masters in art history,
deplored her acts of defacing arty stuff,
then telling the jury enough was enough
saw fit to impose a wide exclusion zone.
This meant she'd to leave her city nursing home.
They found a place for her near Blundellsands.
Relieved to see her go, the staff lent hands
to quickly help her pack and put her on the bus.
She spent the journey wondering, why the fuss?

All she'd done was save the human race,
from having male nudity shoved in their face.
Admittedly she had added to her crimes
by pinching undies from people's washing lines.
And the breaking in and trespass charge
was probably just, but still very harsh.

After the journey had passed Waterloo
she looked out the window, to take in the view.
Her eyes lit up with pleasure, her smile grew
wide.

15

Tingles ran through her with the sight she'd
spied.
Gran sat bolt upright, rubbed her hands with
glee;
a line of naked men, all looking out to sea.

Ashes to ashes

The inspiration for this short piece was the installation by John King of suitcases on Hope Street, Liverpool, entitled 'A Case History.'

As he waited in the doorway of the old warehouse, he remembered a conversation he'd had with his uncle, one night, as a young child. He could picture it vividly.

'Why does the moon remind you of the Bone Man, Uncle Frank?'

Frank, face hidden from the moonlight, had cast a faint shadow on the bedroom wall.

'They slipped into Liverpool on small ships, steered by the light of the moon. The human cargo had endured rough and stormy seas, many were left weakened by the journey. Promised a better life. As they disembarked the Bone Man lined them up in the moonlight, segregated the healthy from the weak. The weak were unpaid, worked to death. Cheap labour. The healthy were herded to a warehouse at the dock.'

Frank made a slashing motion, with his hand on his neck.

'He sold their organs for research, stored their bones in trunks. That was how he was discovered. The sculpture outside your house is in memory of the dead.'

James still felt the nausea rise in his stomach, even though he'd later discovered that the sculpture, 'A Case History', was nothing to do with the Bone Man.

The story was real though, and it had started again.

In the police he was put on the team investigating the trafficking, disappearances, murders, mutilations, every clue led to a dead end.

17

For years it had given him sleepless nights, then came a lightbulb moment, sparked by something his wife had said after vacuuming their hall.

He knew he should mention his suspicions to another officer, but if he was wrong...

He saw the lights go out, waited ten minutes to make sure the building would be empty, before breaking a window to get in.

He was about to vomit into his handkerchief, when Frank found him snooping in his workshop. Frank made ash from bones.

'Why, Frank?'

'Ash is saleable, it has so many uses. No point trying to hide the bones.'

He picked up a carving knife and lunged at his nephew.

James still had the smell of burning in his nostrils as he stepped into their hall, closing the front door behind him. He brushed down his jacket, and checked the carpet for ash, it wouldn't do for his wife to notice it when she vacuumed this time.

18

One Fine Place

Inspired by the name plate on the gate post of a house.

One fine place,
That's all I asked for,
A room to sleep in,
A kitchen and a lounge for rest;

Just a garden to call my own.
A fine place to call my home.

A toad I rescued
And gave a kiss to,
Became a prince
In front of my very eyes.

Then with me being too old to marry
Granted my wish and left in a hurry.

One fine place
Too big to manage
All by myself
Too much to clean.

Huge house, acres of land to tend
So now, with live in staff I depend.

Too many people
All I want is privacy.
Too much to run,
No rest for me.

For sale: would suit a prince's palace,
All I want for myself is one fine place.

For the love of Rosie

Three things happened that morning.

I broke a glass. The CD player started playing on its own. A picture fell off the wall.

The broken glass had been my own fault. I was washing the dishes and my hand had lost its grip on my favourite James Herriot Border Collie mug, letting it fall in to the bowl. The glass had been the casualty not, thankfully, my mug. However the time taken to empty the bowl and carefully gather up the broken pieces had delayed me.

I was filling up the washing bowl for the second time when I heard music. Turning around I was astonished to find the CD had started up on its own and was playing my Duffy CD, the one I thought I had left in my old car when I part exchanged it for my new one. She was singing about her love for her dog and the words stirred up my emotions and I stood at the sink and cried.

I eventually managed to finish the washing up and still puzzling over the mystery of the spontaneous music I went upstairs to the bedroom to get ready for my walk. I kept my outdoor and walking clothes in my husband's section of the wardrobe. His wardrobe was sectioned off better than mine and the empty spaces he had left behind, after he had packed his clothes and left, looked better filled.

I was just choosing a pair of walking trousers from the rail when I heard a loud clatter from downstairs.

'Now what?' I said aloud. 'Am I never going to get that walk today?'

Although dreading what I would find, I didn't act immediately, instead I took my time getting dressed.

'To be honest,' I said to Jean on the phone later

that day, 'I probably took longer deliberately because I felt that something was trying to send me a message. You know what I'm like. Three things all connected with dogs... Yes, Jean , the picture was the one that Mum cross-stitched for me with a farm and a Border Collie and sheep...'

I changed my normal walking route that day. I had been delayed by almost an hour in the end and I didn't want to risk it being dark on the last leg of the walk because of the busy traffic along the dark country lanes at peak hour. So instead of turning left at the end of the drive I turned right towards Pendle Hill.

The day was pleasant. Despite the absence of any sun behind the clouds, there was still the feeling of the spring approaching and the young fresh green leaves and shoots were a welcome sight amongst the dead and rotting leaves and bare twigs left over from the extremely wet winter.

I kept up a steady pace for the first couple of miles, timing my progress between landmarks. This had become a habit since I had started walking alone. It made me focus on my pace and surroundings and stopped me thinking of Rossti. It took me forty five minutes to walk to Gisburn, knocking five minutes off my previous best time.

As I passed 'The Deli' I waved to Susan through the window. She mimed 'a cup of tea?' To me but I pointed to my watch and shook my head. It was very tempting but I knew once I sat with a cup of tea and the daily newspapers in the cosy interior of The Deli I wouldn't continue with my walk, and I needed the routine of a set weekly timetable.

I carried on walking up the road towards Barrowford. It was a strenuous trek but the views were beautiful. There was a steady stream of cars rushing past and with the absence of a pavement, I turned off the main road and followed the footpath signs to Downham. Part way along the road I climbed a stile to take me across the fields. I almost slipped in mud as I put my foot down on the other side, and I quickly grabbed the fence post to right myself. With nothing hurt but my pride I carried on walking but kept my eyes to the ground.

I heard barking. Startled, I looked up and running towards me was a Border Collie baring its teeth. I knew that look, it was more defensive than aggressive. The collie looked very familiar. The same white stripe down the face. Three white socks and a white breast with the tell-tale white tipped tail held in the air. I felt the blood rush to my head and my heart beat faster, making me feel sick.

I ran a few yards towards it and shouted out.

"Rossti."

Then I stopped.

This wasn't Rossti. Of course it couldn't be Rossti. But...

To my amazement the collie's mood changed from defensive to delighted and he bounded over to me, circled me then sat down a couple of yards in front of my feet, panting. Of course it wasn't Rossti. This collie was female for a start, I could see that now, but she continued to sit twitching her body in front of me, just like Rossti used to do when he was waiting expectantly for me to give him a treat or throw the ball or... follow him.

"Hello," I said to her in a voice I used to keep for Rossti. "What do you want?"

I crouched down and held my hand out palm uppermost. She came towards me slowly then put her paw in my hand. Another Rossti trait. She had a name tag so I slowly used my other hand to hold it steady, all the time telling her soothingly what a beautiful girl she was, until I could read it.

"Rosie." I smiled at her. "Well hello, Rosie. No

wonder you came to me, you thought I knew you when I called out a similar name to yours. What do you want, Rosie?"

Rosie removed her paw from my hand, twitched her body and half-turned.

"Show me, Rosie. Show me what you want."

She ran five or six yards ahead of me then crouched down on all fours, head near the ground, as though watching a sheep.

"Go on," I encouraged, "show me."

This time she ran a bit further ahead and repeated the performance.

I picked up a stick and threw it away from her, if she only wanted to play then it would save me deviating from my route. She hesitated for a moment, then ignored it. There was nothing for it but to follow. Rosie was obviously wanting to take me somewhere.

Just as I was beginning to doubt the sanity of my decision to follow a strange dog across muddy fields and through hedgerows, I heard a noise.

Rosie ran ahead of me, barking, then dived through a hedge and out of sight, but I thought I heard a voice shout 'Rosie' as she did so.

I made towards the hedge, and not knowing which way to go next, I shouted.

"Rosie."

A woman's voice replied.

"Hello! Please help, oh please help me."

I squeezed through the small gap that Rosie had run through easily, scratching my face and hands on the branches. Then came to an abrupt halt.

On the other side of the hedge was a ditch and the banks of it were extremely muddy.

"Oh, thank goodness."

To my left, an elderly lady was lying at a very awkward angle in the mud, at the bottom of the ditch. She was pale-faced and had obviously been crying; I could see the muddy streaks from her eyes down her cheeks, left by her tears.

She held out her hand to me and I clambered and slid down the banks, making slow progress with my feet sinking in the stagnant, smelling mud, and carefully made my way along to where she lay.

When I reached her I took her by the hand which was still held out in my direction, and gave it a reassuring squeeze

"Can you move at all, apart from this arm?"

"No, dear, not my legs. The pain is really unbearable." She started to cry again.

As I reached in my pocket for my mobile phone, we made our introductions.

"I am going to phone for an ambulance, May." I told her. I glanced at the signal on my phone and breathed a sigh of relief. Although not a good signal at least I had one. More often than not on my walks locally I was cut off from any network.

I gave the emergency services the best description of the location as I could and described May's situation, with May prompting me. "Probably best to send out the air ambulance?" I added, looking at the distance from the road and the obstacles between a vehicle and the ditch.

The operator's voice on the end of the phone said, "The paramedics will decide about the air ambulance when they assess the injuries and situation. Don't worry. Keep the lady as warm and comfortable as you possibly can and we will get an ambulance out to you.

I glanced up to make doubly sure that there were no trees to impede a helicopter's blades or obvious lakes of water in the field that might disguise a big dip in the level of the ground.

"Thank you," I said to the operator and before I put my mobile back in my pocket, May moaned in pain. "Please be quick, she is lying in such cold wet mud."

Having put my phone back in my pocket I turned my attention to May. Rosie lay next to her. I took off my jacket and placed it over the pair of them in the hope that it would trap the warmth of Rosie's body under the fabric and help keep May warmer.

"She is a lovely dog." I stroked Rosie with my free hand. "How old is she? Have you had her long?"

"She was my husband's dog. He bought her seven years ago, as a pup, from a farmer who breeds them to train as working dogs. She didn't have the right qualities for training up, or something, so he wanted rid. My Bill, being soft, fell in love with her and brought her home. He trained her to be obedient and she followed him everywhere. It was like some sort of mutual admiration bond. She pined for a long time when he died."

May groaned again. The pain was creasing her face and I looked up, willing the ambulance to come into sight.

"We are probably easier reached by the Clitheroe ambulance, than the Yorkshire one." I commented, just for something to say to keep the conversation going. "I suppose it will come from that direction." I pointed in a vague direction of south, south west.

May looked at me.

"I am surprised she befriended you and let you stroke her so readily. She doesn't normally like strangers. How did you know her name?"

"I didn't. For a moment I thought she was my Border Collie, Rossti. She must have thought I called her by her name when I called her Rossti, or maybe she was just so happy to see someone who could help you, that she welcomed me."

"Is your Rossti out walking with you today?" May asked, trying to look around. She gave a moan as the movement pained her. "He didn't follow you. Have you lost him? Is that why you called out to Rosie?"

I shook my head. "I don't have Rossti anymore." I told her. A lump came to my throat.

May looked downcast.

"I can't look after her as well as my Bill did. She needs a lot of exercise and I have too much arthritis in hands and legs to be out walking and playing with her. My knees aren't what they used to be. That's how I ended up in this ditch. I bent down to pick up the ball and my knees just gave on me and I fell forward. There was nothing to reach for, or grab hold of, and I just kept falling and..."

May winced and cried out. She squeezed my hand and I tried changing the subject.

"Where do you live, May? Is it far from here?"

"Rimington, dear. I live in Rimington." Her eyes closed tight for a few seconds. Do you live around here? I haven't seen you before.

"I live—" I heard a siren. "Oh, May. This could be coming for you now." I said cheerfully, although I didn't feel cheerful. May was so pale and had a faint blue tinge around her lips. "Can you hear it?"

"I hope so, dear," she said faintly. I was really worried about her worsening condition. "I live alone. Who will look after Rosie"

"I will," I volunteered without hesitation. "It's so lonely without my Rossti, that Rosie will be some company for me until you are back home and able to manage her."

"How long have you been on your own?"

"Well, Rossti died of kidney failure four months ago. He was fourteen years old. I still expect him to be there each morning and greet me when I come home from the shops. My husband, Paul, left over a year ago so the house is really quiet. Rosie will be fine with me. You needn't worry. I could give..."

I spied a paramedic car on a distant lane and scrambled to my feet. I needed to attract attention to our position. I thought quickly, I was wearing a red jumper, but was that enough to make me stand out? May cried out to me. Then I had an idea. I took my phone out of my pocket and turned the flashlight on. I moved away from the hedge to a more open position and waved the flash light in the direction of the approaching car with one hand and swung the jumper around my head with the other. Rosie, possibly sensing what I was trying to do started barking.

"Good girl," I shouted to her, then following her lead I started shouting too. "Help! Over here! Help!"

It seemed like an age before the car spotted me, but all my jigging about with the shouting and barking must have done the trick as the car pulled to a stop and a paramedic got out.

He made slow progress over the fields through the mud, and I kept nipping back and forth to watch over May.

I was overcome with relief when the paramedic eventually appeared at my side with his first response bag, and I directed him to May. As we rushed over I told him how I had found her and all that I knew about her.

"Can you keep hold of the dog, please," he said after assessing the situation. "It might not like what I do to its owner."

I found Rosie's lead, attached it and stood back so that the paramedic could see to May.

"Now then, May. How did you get yourself into this mess?"

He checked her blood pressure, pulse and breathing rate then opened his bag and prepared a morphine injection for her, all the while talking to her and asking her questions. He turned to me.

"She said you will take care of the dog. She has no one else. Is that right?"

His mobile phone rang as I nodded confirmation. He answered it. "Hi. Yeah. I'm with her now." He proceeded to identify the best way for the air ambulance to approach the field. I watched as he made May as comfortable as he could. Then I heard the helicopter.

Rosie began to bark, she bared her teeth and snarled as the crew rushed to see to May. I watched the rest of the proceedings from a safe distance trying to calm Rosie. They gave May oxygen put a neck brace on her and splints and very carefully transferred her out of the ditch and into the helicopter. The whole procedure took a lot longer than I had expected considering the severity of her accident and the length of time she had been lying in the awful watery ditch, but thankfully I saw them lift May into the helicopter.

I waited until the air ambulance was out of sight before turning towards home. The paramedic had taken my details off me to give to May and the hospital staff.

"Come on, Rosie." I hugged Rosie, stroked her head and gave her a pat. "It's just you and me now. Come and see my home."

Rosie settled in quickly. She had Rossti's bed and bowls and after having a long sniff around the house she followed me everywhere, just like Rossti used to.

I received a phone call from the hospital the next day. May had asked to see me.

She was drugged with painkillers and in a room on her own but she seemed pleased when I walked towards her, even more so when I showed her a video of Rosie, looking happy in my garden, that I'd taken with my phone.

I didn't stay long but I returned each day until they moved her onto the ward.

There was a light in her eyes and she was full of the gossip from all the patients each time I visited her.

"My garden will be a right mess," she said to me one day. "I can't afford a gardener and my Bill was so proud of his garden that it would break my heart to think I'd let it go to weed."

"I love gardening," I told her. "If you like I could come to visit when you get out of hospital and tidy it up for you. That way I would be able to see Rosie too." I didn't tell May, but I was trying to prepare myself for the day I had to give Rosie back. It would be almost like losing Rossti all over again.

May looked at me in astonishment.

"My dear, I am so sorry. I thought I had told you already. I certainly meant to." I looked at her, not daring to hope. "I want you to have Rosie. I am too old to look after her and I would be fearful of falling again. After all this palaver," she gestured around the room, "I never want to see a hospital ever again."

My eyes filled up, and lost for words, I gave her a huge hug.

"Thank you. Oh May, thank you. I will still do your garden and I will bring Rosie with me so you can have time together while I'm busy."

May smiled and patted my hand. "I'd like that. But you don't have to do the garden all the time, you could just come to chat."

I made arrangements to call at her house the next week and left with a spring in my step.

I knew it was going to be a good day.

That morning I turned on the radio and the first

words I heard were '...then I look at you, and the world's alright with me'. The DJ was playing a Bill Withers song. It had been my husband's favourite in our earlier days. I thought of May's Bill, and hoped he wouldn't mind my messing with his garden and taking care of his dog.

Then there was the second incident.

Before I left the house, Rosie knocked over a pile of papers waiting to be recycled. When I set about clearing them up I found the picture I had searched for since Rossti's death. It was one taken on holiday of me with Rossti and Paul. I was overjoyed to have found it, and it gave me the idea to take one of myself with Rosie as a souvenir. I perched my camera on a table, put it on self-timer and ran over to Rosie. As the camera clicked Rosie leant forward to lick my face. Just as Rossti had done in the photo I'd found.

I opened the door to my car and Rosie leant forward and licked my face again.

"You are going to live with me for good," I told her as I started the ignition. I glanced in the mirror. Rosie was sat in the back seat wearing a wide grin.

As I approached my house I could see someone looking in through my kitchen window. They had their back to me but I could tell it was male. Rosie started to growl.

Alarmed I stopped the car and, leaving the door open, I walked over to see who the guy was.

"What are you doing?"

The intruder turned around.

I gasped and Rosie rushed to my side and barked.

"I didn't think I'd see you for another year."

"Things changed. We finished the contract early and I've got three months' leave, so I thought I'd use it to come and see my best girl."

I hugged him so hard that he caught his breath and laughed. Then we kissed as if it was our first time.

Rosie had stopped barking and was waiting patiently for me to give her some sort of signal.

"So, who is this beautiful girl?"

"Paul meet Rosie. Rosie meet Paul."

Paul got down on his haunches to greet Rosie. Rosie put her paw on his knee and licked his hand.

I had my family together. I brushed away a tear of joy.

The car radio played 'It's going to be a lovely day'.

Lads' night. A Sonnet

When drinking with the lads my plight is plain to see
My thoughts freeze, and here lies my flaw.
They presume I have a meagre repartee
Then they dismiss me as a bore.
It isn't that I try to act the prude
I don't intend to play that role at all
I try not to be misconstrued
But age has dimmed my memory recall.
I vowed to keep a notebook in my pocket
To write in ideas and tales to tell,
A list of deeds I don't want to forget,
To entertain my drinking pals as well.
Still the note pad is unopened, my deeds are small.
I confess to having nothing to confess to, after all.

Train of Thought

The inspiration was a photograph of a man helping a woman get onto a moving tram.

The tutor handed back her final assessment.

"Read my example of a happy-ever-after, again. Then maybe I could meet you after the course to give you some pointers. You show promise."

"No, thanks."

She remembered the corny example.

John jumped across the gap, onto the last carriage. The bomb was set to go off soon. He leant forward to unhitch the carriage from the rest of the train, as he did so he looked straight into her eyes.

"Goodbye, my darling girl. Always remember I loved you."

Her heart lurched as he separated the carriage. It was in that moment she realised if she couldn't be with him, she didn't want to be with anyone else either.

She jumped across the gap to join him.

Bleugh! Her heroine wasn't that stupid. If the hero was daft enough to get himself blown up, then he could do it on his own, she'd find someone else.

She packed away her laptop, tossed her Romance Writers course booklet into the bin on the way out of the room, heard the tutor call her name, but carried on walking.

"Wait!"

She turned, glimpsed the pink briefcase, and quickened her step. How very 'Barbara Cartland'. She would stick to writing crime and thriller novels. Romance was definitely not for her.

The tram was at the platform.

She was aware of her tutor still following as she boarded the last carriage. Then as the tram began to pull away, he shouted to her.

"Don't go! Give me your hand to help me on, I need to see you again. We need to talk."

Something cruel inside her made her reach out, despite having no intention of helping him up. He threw his briefcase at her feet and stretched, almost grasping her hand.

"I've loved you from the moment you joined my class. If I can't be with you, I don't want you to be with anyone else either."

She withdrew her hand, as planned. Then as she looked at the briefcase, the realisation of his words and intention slowly dawned on her.

Nelson

Nan found a one-eyed teddy in a rock pool on the beach. I came across him in a toy box and it inspired this small poem.

My teddy's name is Nelson
Nan found him in the sea
She put him in her pocket
And brought him home for me.

War 1916

When I join my new unit in the Australian field ambulance, division one, it is a huge shock to my young body. The unit is very regimental, more so than my old unit, and I have left my friends, including Billy and Pete, behind. My eighteen-year-old head can't cope with the enormous change without my best friends.

Lonely but not alone, there are 40,000 of us trainees camped along the six or seven-mile stretch of the canal from Tel-el-Kebir. Miles away from home, and separated from my family and friends, I feel isolated and homesick.

A great tiredness sweeps over my body where previously hope and light-hearted camaraderie had lodged. I drag my legs, my shoulders are weighed down, and the nausea for home in the pit of my stomach threatens to force its way into the open every waking hour.

I am about to lie down when the door bursts open.

"We have orders to occupy the reserve trenches against the Bedouin along the canal."

I gasp.

I am not the only one to be alarmed but my mouth is too dry to ask questions.

"Isn't that a bit too close to the action, sir?"

I give Joey a look of gratitude. Thank goodness some of us were able to speak.

"No lad, it's not close to the front line. You won't need your mum. It's quite safe." Some of the lads laugh and Joey looks mortified. With a camp full of testosterone, it doesn't do to show a weakness in emotion or strength.

I run my tongue along my lips but it is barely moist enough to make any difference.

I long for Toowoomba, for my friends Billy,

Pete, Ned and Jack. I yearn to be kissing Doris after the dances.

What am I doing here? Crouching in dirty holes in the ground, sleeping in overcrowded camps with strangers, miles from family and loved ones. For what? For a country on the other side of the world that I have never seen.

I only joined up because I wanted to be a doctor. We thought it would be a lark, a bit of a laugh.

Well, I'm not laughing now.

The homesickness is getting worse. I try to carry on and be brave. I can't appear weak in front of my new unit. After two gruelling route marches of five and seven miles, I start with a fever. I suspect that, at some point, my homesickness has disappeared and instead become an illness. I am convinced that I have mumps.

By the time the fever starts, I have become accustomed to my compatriots in my unit, and don't want to let them down. We are being sent to France and I don't want to miss out or leave them a man short. I can't tell anyone about the mumps.

For the next few days, we make route marches of seven, ten and twelve miles. I am exhausted and at times burn up with the fever. I weaken considerably and am sure that I became so bad it was noticeable. Nobody mentions it and I haven't become close enough to any of the men to confide in them.

The crunch comes when we are forced to route march to Tel-el-Kebir battlefields; this was where Viscount Worsley defeated the Turks in 1882 after his occupation of Egypt. There is excruciating agony in my groin. Beads of sweat run down my temples. My temperature is high and I struggle to complete the march. The sun beats down and the pain gnaws at my head and burns the back of my eyes. The sweat from heat and fever runs down my face, but still I carry on.

I collapse after the parade, and am carried to the hospital on a stretcher where I am examined by the doctor. He confirms my suspicion that I have mumps but I also have the added complication of paratyphoid with a temperature of 103 degrees and rising.

Despite the nursing staff, with the help of the doctors, bathing me night and day with cold baths, my temperature swings from 105 to 103 and back again. For two days, I lie at death's door, dipping in and out of this life and the next. At one point, I awake to hear a doctor say he would be surprised if I made it through the night.

I fill with anger.

I'm going to let mumps defeat me. No man was thought a hero dying from mumps. If I join my unit going to France, even in my weakened state I could still fight. If I lose my life in active service my family could hold their heads up at home. I have to get out of the hospital.

My break comes when I have a visit from my two friends. I hear a familiar voice.

"Charlie, how are you, matey?"

I open my eyes.

"Bill. Can you get me out of here?"

"You'll leave here soon enough."

"I need to..."

"Can you walk?"

I try to walk but am too weak, and my legs just crumple under me.

Bill rubs his chin and mutters something to Pete who nods.

Next thing I know they have borrowed a stretcher and smuggle me out of the hospital. How on earth they manage to get me past the nurses at the bottom of the ward and through the camp, but they do.

We board the train under cover of darkness and leave Tel-el-Kebir after midnight. I have a bad time in the open wagon. I can't get warm and have to fight from being pulled into a dark abyss. Once or twice I catch Bill and Pete exchanging looks and nods. I presume they think me foolish and probably a burden to my unit, but my pride will not let me give up. Again it occurs to me that it is unusual that nobody has stopped us boarding the train.

After an uncomfortable night, we arrive at Alexandria. With Bill on one side and Pete on the other, practically holding me up, we march to the wharf to board the Kingstonian which is to take us to France.

Escorted by two cruisers, we move out of Alexandria harbour. I hear orders being given to collect our life belts and wear them all day and sleep with them under our heads at night.

Bill is reluctant to take me down to the deck, again he exchanges glances with Pete.

"For goodness' sake, Bill. What's with all the secret nods and looks? I'll be fine by the time we get to France. Now let's get those safety belts."

Officers are calling out the names off a roll call, and handing each man who answered a life belt. I hear Ned's name being called and try to attract his attention, but he ignores me. Hurt by his lack of acknowledgement, I turn back to Bill and Pete. They shuffle their feet awkwardly but say nothing.

I wait.

My name isn't called.

I carry on waiting. The officer doesn't even look

up at me, and starts to put away his notes.

I realise he is going to walk off without an explanation.

"Oi, Sir!"

No response.

It dawns on me then that Bill and Pete haven't been given a lifebelt either. Neither of them seem bothered that their names haven't been called out.

"What's going on?"

They don't answer. Bill turns away, and Pete sticks his hands in his pockets and looks down. I repeat my question. Bill is the first to speak.

"Didn't you think it odd when we appeared by your bedside?"

"Odd? You are my friends. Why should it be odd that you came to see me?"

"Mate..." Bill doesn't finish. The officer appears on deck and is walking towards us. Bill and Pete stand together, each holding a hand up to me in farewell, and fade from my vision.

I hardly hear the officer, so astonished am I at their disappearance.

"What are you doing out here? Where is your belt?"

"My friends..."

"What friends? Your name!"

I give my name and this time it is the officer's turn to be surprised. He checks the list from his pocket for my details.

My name has been crossed off as 'invalided out'.

I ask about Bill and Pete. Their names have never been on the list. I try to remember a detail, but fail. All I know is, thanks to the appearance of Bill and Pete, I am where I want to be.

I am ordered to see the doctor.

Plumber's Mate

My drains were smelling in the heat of summer
So phoned 'DrainO'block' to send out a plumber.
I recognised the back of his bum on the floor
He turned, I knew straight away I'd met him before.
We chatted as he worked, but I can't pretend
I was bowled over, when he cleared my u-bend.
Though I knew we had something worth pursuing,
And while I watched him set about gluing
The joints, I asked him for a date, saw him blush,
He accepted so quickly, I felt a hot flush.

We make an odd couple, he's short and I'm lanky
He wipes his nose on his sleeve, I use a hanky
I hail from West Lancs, he's Scouse as they come.
I look like Olive Oil, he looks like Tom Thumb.
I talk far too much, he's quiet 'cause he stutters,
At the end of the day, really none of that matters.
We got on fine. You can't describe him as hot,
But I'm desperate, and single and like him a lot.
He is scruffy, beer-bellied, and barely luke warm,
I'm no model, flat chested, older and worn.

He moved in. Now I always have flushed drains,
A large double water butt for when it rains,
No leaky washers. He fitted a water meter,
I have a new boiler and smart immersion heater.
We don't sizzle or set the bed sheets on fire
Just take my word, it's not all dampened desire.
We have warm snuggly nights, Jacuzzi baths,
Beer, wine, pork scratchings, TV, plenty of laughs.

The house is OUR home now, not his or mine
It will do us quite nicely, until the end of our time.
We share the cooking, chores, company and laughter

41

Together we'll live the dream 'happy ever after'.
As we grow old, I'll always bless that whiffy hot
summer,
When I found my soul mate, in my very own
plumber.

Giving them wings

The inspiration was a black and white photograph of a boy in a fur trimmed hood, sitting by a statue in a square, feeding the pigeons.

The boy waited.

His own banishment did not worry him. His concern lay with the outcome of his argument with the Elders of the district.

He dared to challenge the wisdom behind the district cleansing, caging of the slow-witted, stubborn, impaired and unlovable. They were labelled dirty vermin.

"They have other qualities. Give them time to discover their inner beauty and knowledge. Let them free."

"Who are you to question the decisions of the Elders and the district tradition?"

He broke into their cage at night, left the door open for them to walk free.

The Elders drove him away. Sent him to the city of a hundred tongues, amongst the homeless and the nameless.

The Vermin, determined to find the boy so he could tell them more about their qualities, homed in on his light.

It was not an easy quest. Some stayed behind, nervous about what lay ahead. The rest followed the path of his flight. They negotiated labyrinths of temptations, pain and gluttony. They braved storms, abuse, rejection and predators.

Some fell away, weakened by the journey, others found death waiting for them. It was a difficult search, even for the strong amongst them, but still they ploughed on.

Close to the fetid vagrants with sleeping bags, but far removed from the suited and brief-cased, the boy sat on the steps of the square. He heard calls and raised his head.

His lips parted into a wide smile, his obvious delight showed clearly on his face.

One by one they appeared.

All of the remaining Vermin found enlightenment, as he predicted they would.

Each had learnt their qualities and value to society along the way.

They delivered, to the boy, their gifts of love, unity, truth, understanding, determination, loyalty, faithfulness and above all experience and wisdom.

Their self-discovery gave them wings.

The Turning of Autumn

She watched faeries in their finery, twinkling and
dancing in the night sky.
He glimpsed planets, millions of light years away,
because science is fact not fancy.

She reached up to draw down the moon, and
danced in the moonlight.
He reached up to draw down the blinds, he
couldn't sleep in the moonlit room.

She skipped across the lawn between the
toadstools and faerie rings.
He moaned that the lawn needed aerating, and
raked up all the fungi.

She chased the white unicorns crashing onto the
shore, and raced barefoot over the dust of
mermaids.
He gave her an account of the amount of
pollutants in the oceans, and cursed the sand
creeping into his shoes and socks.

She laughed and told him to lighten up.
He scowled and told her to grow up.

She pressed the golden leaves of Autumn, and
collected the beads of giants, as an offering for
the Mabon Goddess.
He cursed the falling leaves, littering the paths
and garden, and scoffed at her creative
arrangement of dying leaves and wrinkled
conkers.

By the next fall, her breasts, that had once
suckled new life, were puckered and decaying,
with tumours the size of giants beads.

45

She saw Angels in the white feathers that floated past the window.
He swore at the moulting pigeons, messing up his patio.

She saw wings, spread out, and hands reaching down to grasp hers and take her peaceful, trusting soul up to theirs.
He saw hands reaching out to shake his, and the box that held her beautiful body, lowered down.

He watched, with misty eyes, the twinkling faeries in the night sky.
He reached to touch her face in the moon, and yearned to see her dancing once more in the moonlight.

He sat amongst the toadstools, and wished on the faerie rings, dug his feet into the dust of mermaids and let the roar of the crashing unicorns, cascading on the shore, drown his howls of anguish.

In the autumn he pressed the golden leaves and putting them on his bedside table, added them to his growing collection of white feathers.

Frost Giants

This was inspired by a friend's piece of experimental art work. It appeared to me to have a half open eye in the centre

Awake, awake, the sun is losing her touch.
Weakened by Winter's thrust
she recoils.

Then while she sleeps and leaves the earth
unguarded,
The freezing air started
it's turmoil.

The frost Giants, awake from their light slumbers,
One by one, their numbers
ice uncoil.

Then lay it on low ground, hill, water and leaf.
Glisten, shimmer, glass sheath.
nature's foils

Their waking brings long sleep, death or winter
bleak.
Icy breath pinches cheek.
Life embroils

Sun returns. They fade to sleep, their work
complete.
Spring rebirths. Life repeats,
nurtures, toils.

The Princess and The Dragon

I hear the crunch of slate and gravel, and slowly open one sleepy eye.

My body is tired and it takes me a while to realise that the sound is coming towards me.

I sleep a lot more these days and by the approaching sound of the crunching slate and shuffling gravel, it appears that I have forgotten it is the day of St Ivor, or why else would one of the townsfolk dare to come near my lair?

I must be getting old. Wearily, I lift my head.

Hang on a minute!

Why is it so quiet?

Have I slept through all the reverie and festive binge drinking, the sports with fireworks? Surely not.

I struggle to open my eyes fully, so deep was my sleep. Why won't they stop this nonsense? It is 2999; in six months it will be the new millennium.

Making her way towards me is not some luckless girl chosen by the villagers, but the Princess Terrwyn herself. There are no villagers watching her progress up the mountain and I am not surprised, because it is not yet sunrise. I know now it is not St Ivor's day.

She walks with her shoulders slumped, most unlike her. I hold Princess Terrwyn in high regard; she has more fire in her belly than the Diffyn-gwr (King's Guard) and is braver than all of her father's court, so seeing her walk without her usual aura of proud spirit puzzles me.

I wait until she is within range, then send her a warning flame.

She stirs from her thoughts and stands straight-backed, legs slightly apart but firm.

Ah, her spirit is awake.

Her body language shouts 'stubborn'.

"You don't frighten me." she says.

"I don't?"

"No. I have watched you for years."

Then we have both watched each other. This could be interesting.

"And what did you see?" I didn't mean to spit, but as I spoke I showered her with sparks.

She stays in her same position, back straight, trousered legs firm and attitude defiant. No, she definitely isn't afraid of me, she doesn't even flinch.

"I saw a way to a better life."

She's smart too. I play along.

"What did you see?"

"I saw a way out of our town. I saw a chance to escape the suitors my father chooses for me. I saw freedom."

"Yes?"

There is a pause.

"You are the key to my freedom."

"And how do you suppose I become that key?"

I raise myself up to my full height and in doing so I spy a figure running clumsily in our direction.

Terrwyn spins around to see what has attracted my attention.

"I don't believe it!" She turns to me. "See! See what I have to put up with. My father will have sent him. I can't move in this awful town without someone telling my father." This time she moves her foot, only to stamp it down hard on the slate, sending splinters into the air. "Oh. I might have known; a noble knight." She spits on the ground.

I like the girl. I like her a lot. The princess has mettle.

"Princess Terrwyn, your father has sent me to save you."

"You needn't bother! Go back to my father and tell him you were too late."

There is something about this knight that I do not like. He does not show any fear, he has not even glanced in my direction. I experience a warning rush of fire to the throat and my chest burns. As I listen to them, I take in the knight's appearance.

"Your father, the King, has decreed that whoever rescues you from the dragon..." – he still doesn't so much as glance in my direction – "... shall inherit his kingdom and marry you. So I've come to take you back."

I can smell rotten vegetables mixed with bad hygiene. A memory awakens inside my head but I can't bring it to the fore.

She points to me. "This is 2999, you are supposed to be extinct." She turns back to the knight. "And as for you, you should get a real job. Do you think I want to be a part of all this stupid nonsense? Grow up!"

I watch the knight arrest a scowl on his face, and twist it into a sneer.

"I like a girl who's masterful. I will do you a deal then, princess: you give me a kiss and I will leave you alone. I won't claim the lands and fortune. I will walk away and let you fight your own battles. How about it?"

The princess laughs. Despite her brave and boyish façade, her laugh is hypnotic, like sweet music cascading over smooth rocks in a stream. I am mesmerised and caught off guard for I have taken my eyes off the knight, and in that careless moment he has already lunged at the princess.

The memory bursts in my head like shards of glass from a smashed bottle.

A troll. A fetid recluse from the Snowdon region! My jaw opens to roar; a split second too late. Before she can struggle, he has gripped her and planted his mouth over hers for that kiss.

The world turns into slow motion.

Horrified, I watch as her tanned freckled skin sprouts white hairs and her small frame bends slowly until she is on all fours. Her feet become hoofs and scrape wilfully against the stone, her ears point upright, her small tail points down and all the time she is bleating.

The knight is indeed a troll; moss and mould in his tangled hair, ugly lumpy skin, fat nose, jagged teeth and the smell of a ripe cesspit.

Anger burns as a tight ball in the furnace inside me. I pull myself up to my full height as the ball of fire pushes its way up my neck and out through my mouth and nose. The troll picks up Terrwyn and holds her close to his body. I divert my head quickly to avoid burning the princess as well as the troll, and the flames fall to the side of the triumphant troll, who shakes a fist in the air.

"Losing your touch, pyro-boy."

The troll backs away with his hostage still shielding him from an attack by fire. Smoking madly, I launch my heavy but cumbersome frame in his direction, and by some spectacular gymnastic moves, manage to swing my tail around behind him. Such is the momentum generated from my base and along the length of my tail that the lash from whipping it builds up, knocking the lumbering Troll forwards.

He releases her goat form as he falls and she takes her chance to leap off and scramble along the loose chippings, out of his reach.

I hurl a firestorm of large hungry flames, and they rain down on the troll.

He gives a long, loud, piercing cry as he grabs my tail and sinks his teeth into it.

The effect is instant.

The numbness spreads like freezing tendrils from the bite.

51

My wings open to take flight. I hover over the running fireball and rain down more flames in an avalanche of rapid fire until, suddenly weak, I fall to the ground. The troll hurtles down the mountainside and out of sight.

I have failed.

I should have finished him off; only if the troll dies will the princess be released from the goat's body.

I drag my tail back into my lair and inspect it.

Stone! My tail is turning to stone and soon my body will follow. I can't stop it. It is beyond my capabilities.

The princess trots over to me and licks my tail.

"It's no use." I shake my head and point to the back of the cave.

"Go through the cave. At the end, on the other side of the mountain, is Blaneau Grogau. The townsfolk there will look after you."

She steps towards the back of my lair and turns to look at me.

"I'm sorry, Princess."

She nods and trots off.

The cold freezes my tail and creeps up my back.

I close my eyes.

I awake to the sound of fireworks, and karaoke singing assaults my ears.

Oh for goodness sake. Not again!

Someone, somewhere, is screeching a god-awful rendition of 'I Will Go On'. I lift a clawed foot to keep out the assault on my ears.

No claws.

No scales.

I look down. No tail!

Standing a few feet away from me is Terrwyn.

"The troll died?"

She nods.

I look down at my ragged clothes and dusty old body. My eyes are drawn to a glistening mark on my shoulder in the shape of a teardrop. It's not true love's kiss but it was good enough to transform me.

"Did you expect a handsome prince?"

She is smiling.

"Sorry to disappoint you."

She links my arm.

"It's better this way. We can just be friends." She gives me a playful punch in the ribs. "I don't want a boyfriend, if you get my drift." She winks at me.

I am grinning. It is a wide grin showing off centuries-old teeth.

"Suits me. It is the year 2999 after all. I predict there will be big changes in the next millennium. Even in Llemwynw!"

A voice of authority rises above the revelries and reaches our ears. We both look down.

The wind snatches some of the words, but we both know the gist of the speech.

"Blah blah, St. Ivor's Day, blah blah, a young girl chosen... to the dragon. This is 2999, a momentous occasion for any young girl. They will go down in legend as the last girl sacrificed in this century... Blah blah, an honour..."

"Come on, I'm tired of all this nonsense." She guides me to the back of my lair and I follow willingly.

We stand together on the other side, looking over at Blaneau Grogau and its green hills with a river, sparkling like a crystal snake, winding down to the sea, before we start on the steep path down.

I Did It My Way

I overheard part of a conversation on the train, and it became my inspiration for this piece of flash fiction. I'm not telling you which bit I overheard though!

"I'm sure it is."

"Believe me sweetheart, if I say it isn't possible; it isn't."

He was getting on my nerves, big time. We were supposed to be collaborating on a script for a television series. The deadline was looming and every contribution I made he shot down in his superior, sneering, way that made him unpopular amongst the rest of the group.

I gritted my teeth, spoke from between them.

"It stays in. I insist."

His laugh rumbled inside his huge belly, like some ancient clanging boiler, then exploded from his wide, ugly mouth. The exertion from this scornful act of ridicule, caused sweat to drip from his forehead. As he leant forward to grope in his trouser pocket for a handkerchief to wipe his face, a few drops of sweat landed on my cheek.

A whole year of anger therapy rapidly unravelled in my head.

I sprung to my feet.

My full five foot, one inch frame, brought me level with his shiny round head, despite him being seated.

"Sweetheart, we all know, if it were possible you wouldn't be in this group with us petty criminals. We are writing 'True Crimes' not fairy stories. The Judge and jury decided it wasn't physically possible for someone of your petite size to break the neck of that heavyweight boxer. All the evidence showed how ridiculous the suggestion was."

"Are you sure about that?"

I lunged at him.

His bulky frame was slow to move.

I had my arm around his neck; his eyes were bulging, his tongue lolled from between his swollen lips. I placed my lips near to his ear while he could still hear me.

"I had the best solicitor."

The crack of bones was satisfying.

I finished the script; my way.

Flibbertigibbet

She entered the ballroom floor, with a smile
Looked all around to make sure we were
watching.
Poised for the music, head held high,
Toe pointed, then she started her dancing.
She whirled and swirled,
Bounced and flounced.
That flibbertigibbet.
With Nell Gwyn neckline, tattoo on her shoulder,
Her gypsy style dress moved as she swayed.
Her partners, agile men who were older.
Each tune, another dance to the audience she
played.
She whirled and swirled,
Bounced and flounced
That flibbertigibbet
Kept up the pace for three hours, on a packed
floor,
Bosom heaving, bottom rounded and fleshy.
She entertained, knew all the dances and more,
Agile, light on her feet, rippling and swishy.
She whirled and swirled,
Bounced and flounced
That flibbertigibbet

Through the old time she romptied and
pomptied,
Straight backed, stately, knees up but jolly.
Through Latin, arms expressive, she shimmied,
Head turning, legs long, steps quickly and slowly.
She whirled and swirled,
Bounced and flounced
That flibbertigibbet
In Jive, high kicks, moving and rocking she
titillates,

Jiggled and swivelled, shook her boobs to the
song.Teasing in tango, with sexy moves she
scintillates,
Foxtrot was smooth, seamless turning, gliding
along.
She whirled and swirled
Bounced and flounced
That flibbertigibbet
Then when the organ disappeared in the ground
She applauded and beamed at the crowd,
Skipped from the floor, cheeky wave all around,
She picked up her crutches, then hobbled off out.
That flibbertigibbet.

The Antique Emporium

"I won't be long."

"I've heard that before. We don't need any more rubbish, Ali, the house is full of it. If you didn't spend so much on junk we would have enough to book a break in Venice or Rome or..."

I hear them whisper to me, and quicken my steps.

"Spend hours walking aimlessly around streets in my heels." I throw the words over my shoulder. "Days listening to you spout word-for-word from the tourist guide. Blisters on my feet. No thanks, Geoff."

The whispers grow more urgent.

I push my hand in my bag and touch my purse. My hands tingle.

I hear a rustle here, a sigh there.

"You think more of your junk than you do of me."

I stop listening to Geoff; instead I focus on the treasures ahead, my hands burning up with the desire to spend on someone's discarded treasure.

The murmurings increase.

I follow them.

A large willow pattern jug attracts my attention. I have one like it and bend to look inside. Aunt Doris made lemonade, with proper lemons, in a jug just like this one. I gaze at it fondly remembering, with a slight smile, visits to my aunt on warm summer days and sweet sticky glasses of homemade lemonade.

There's a hiss. No, not a hiss: a swish.

A softly-spoken word draws me towards a long fur coat on the vintage clothing stand. I stroke it tenderly. The memory of my Nan's fur coat is rubbing a hand against my heart. I sniff it, hoping for the scent of Lily of the Valley, my Nan's chosen perfume, but it smells musty. I miss you, Nan. Eyes pricking with tears, I move on through the stalls.

The chattering continues.

It dances around me, sometimes to my right, sometimes to my left, but always chattering. Far off voices buzzing in my ears.

I stop at a shelf of postcards. Holiday memories; most so typically British describing the weather, but some with private cryptic messages and words of love. I am slowly flipping through them when I hear a tobacco tin and pipe, just like Grandpa's, call to me in a low soft voice. It is a wonder that I can hear the faint tones because the whispers circulating behind me are growing in number, louder and louder begging me to turn around, but I ignore them. Thoughts of Grandpa make my stomach flutter and I lift the tin and pipe to my nose, closing my eyes to inhale the memories. I want to linger, remembering winters snuggled up on the couch next to Grandpa, in front of a roaring fire. But no matter how hard I try to bring forward more memories I'm prevented from doing so by the incessant mumblings and calls from over my shoulder.

Mesmerised, I allow myself to be lured towards the calling and promises of a treasure trove.

I ignore stalls of bric-a-brac, instead I follow the louder calls and mutterings coming from a stall in the far corner, when I step into it, it's like being transported into my home. I gaze in wonder at what appears to be a mirror of my own life. How can this be? I walk further into the unit gently touching an elephant ornament here, a teapot there. A pair of white angel bookends, the same as those on my mantelpiece at home, draw me further in.

How odd.

Was it a coincidence that the stallholder had collected bits and pieces from different places to make up this collection; or had they cleared a house somewhere, and it was that owner who had the same taste as me?

What are the chances of that?

I walk around gently touching an ornament or two, hesitating at souvenirs that I had forgotten about until now, mentally placing each piece in its position at home.

Then I spy it.

The reason my instinct led me to this stall.

Last month, after an argument with Geoff about the amount of time and money I spent amassing my collection, or "rubbish" as he calls it, I slammed the door of the lounge. The vibration caused a figurine to jump from the shelf and smash into hundreds of pieces on the wood floor.

I feel a sharp tingle of excitement as I am drawn towards the furtive whispers emitting from the identical figurine. It's in perfect condition on a shelf between a Mucha clock and a Mauchline ware sewing box. I can't believe my luck. I reach out and pick it up.

The minute I touch the figurine, I'm aware of a whooshing noise and I spin around to see where it is coming from.

The stall unit is encased in glass.

I'm trapped.

There is no door.

No way out.

I peer through the glass looking for someone to help me. There's no one around. Vicious words spew from the figurine, spiteful contemptuous jeers. I release my hold and it falls to the floor, but doesn't break.

The air in the unit changes and I gasp as my throat dries and tightens.

60

I'm being pulled and pushed, turned this way and that. My clothes are being tugged from my back. I hold on to them, clutching them, and scream and scream. Now I am being pummelled and my hands are wrenched apart, releasing my jacket. I cannot see my attacker but somehow I manage to reach the glass and for a moment I'm free of the assailant.

Hammering at the glass I shout, "Help me, please help me."

My hands ache from the constant blows against my prison and my knuckles bleed, but still I keep hammering and banging on the glass for someone to come to my rescue.

My breath is escaping in rapid gasps. My pulse races. The tugging and pulling starts again. As I shake with the tremors, Geoff appears. He is obviously searching the building, looking for me.

"Oh thank God! Geoff!"

I attack the glass with renewed strength, hammering and kicking at it with all the power I can summon. I ignore the venom spitting from behind. I don't realise that its sound is retreating. I am shouting, "Geoff!", but he can't hear me.

Wait! No! What's he doing with her?

"Geoff! Geoff! That's not me."

My heart is assaulting my ears, deafening me.

She's wearing my coat. She's wearing my clothes!

My legs, leaden and weak, collapse under me. I'm on my knees. I claw at the glass, hoarse with shouting. Geoff smiles at her. I watch as that heinous thing smiles back and gazes lovingly up at Geoff. Then to my horror I can hear her.

"Why do I need any of this rubbish? You're right, Geoff. Let's go and book that weekend in Venice."

I scream as Geoff kisses her, but it dies in my

throat.

"No, don't go, Geoff! Don't leave me here."

I have no voice left. The tears spill from my eyes then freeze on my cheeks. My body is stiff. Geoff walks off with the identical me.

I have no choice but to watch from my place on the shelf between the Mucha clock and the Mauchline Ware sewing box.

My Husband's Eyes. A Sonnet

My Husband's eyes are red and bloodshot in the
sun,
His belly full of beer he had last night.
His nose and chest are rather too well done,
But I remain unmovéd by his plight.
The Costa Brava was his choice this year.
The drink is cheap and flows all day and night,
And whilst he has more than his fill of beer,
I become increasingly uptight.
At last he finishes his pint and snoozes,
I wish for hills and walks in Italy
Away from rowdy Brits and boozers,
A more romantic break, for him and me.
As I plan our next year in Lake Garda,
His nose burns, and mouth open, he snores
harder.

Betula and Ulmus

An article in a nature book about Dutch Elm Disease and its accompanying picture prompted the inspiration for this piece of flash fiction.

She tossed her hair in the icy wind.

While Jack Frost had played at painting patterns on her slender form, and the ground around her, she had covered Ulmus, protecting him from the weather's worst elements. Already much weakened from wounds, he had suffered many falls.

Unfolding, and rising from her hands and knees Betula faced Ulmus and surveyed the damage the ravaging winter had done to his fragile form.

His long battle with Scolytus in the summer had taken much of the life out of him. By the autumn his strength had all but wilted; he became hollow. His scars from the battle still streaked and spotted his otherwise tough torso.

Lovingly Betula leant towards him and reaching out her limbs to gently touch him, sought to unlock his pain so Ulmus' sap might rise again, in the hope they may last another year together.

Daughter of Hades

'Dreamer, dream on whilst I pull you deeper, then
down.
Lying on my mat of moss, grass, heather and
peat.
Innana's gifted a red stream, made you complete,
Innocent child, now into a woman you've grown.'

Darkening moon, bringing with it birth's healing
flow.
He watches, waiting, it's time to beckon her in.
Into his lifeless kingdom for life to begin.
Dreamer stay dreaming, alert not the crow.

'Lie still while I touch you, ignore the hounds'
baying.
Eyes see not the shadows of miserable dreams.
My heart on your heart, my ribs on your ribs, hot
streams
Of my life meeting yours. New awakening.'

Dreamer dream on, return to your own world and
rest.
Dwell not on what was, but will be, before the
spring.
Pacts, promise of sharing, your body is changing.
Hush now young woman, hush now stay sleeping
'till blessed.
ShhhHHHHhhhhhhhh......

'Dream on dreamer, dear beautiful daughter of
mine.
I will keep watch over you, see you through the
night,
Blind the crow's eyes 'till your return at morning
light.

Your father awaits. You're mine for a meagre time.'

All night she worries, rocks back and forth by the bed.
She prays her daughter remembers to heed her words;
Eat none of their food, drink no drink while you are there.
Return before the closing gates keep in the dead.

Morning is near, but she hears a frightening sound.
Innana's gift blessed her daughter while she lay sleeping.
Pact fulfilled, bereft, she drank poison, lay weeping,
Waiting to sleep with the dead, deep under the ground.
ShhhhHHHHHHHhhhhhhhh....

Lost In The Storm

The north west coast was lashed with 75 mph gales preceded by driving rain, and Toto made his escape when Shaun left the front door open as he nipped outside the house to send a text.

'Can't meet u 2nite, sorry Eve :(Clare's goin mad bout the storm - worried trees will cum down and thru the babies bedroom- or flyin fence panels will smash windows- she wants me home - wud rather b with u :(xxxxxxx'

He pressed send just as the Cairn Terrier brushed past his legs and off down the road.

Shaun cursed himself for leaving the door open. Toto regularly made a bid for freedom but never went far. It would have been so easy just to pick up his keys and pop them in his pocket, now he was going to have to struggle in the gales to find him.

His mobile phone vibrated in his pocket. He took it out and looked at the screen. 'Leave her'.

He hurriedly grabbed his waterproof jacket and keys, then left the house and turned in the direction he last saw Toto.

"Toto. Toto!" He called. "Here Toto. Good boy."

No sign of Toto.

He forged ahead, turning his face away from the wind. The dust from the fields caught in his eyes and smarted. He put his hand up to shield them.

"Toto! Blast you! This is no time for games. Toto. Where are you?"

He carried on some more until he didn't recognise his surroundings. The dust was playing tricks with his vision. He wished he had thought to bring some treats to tempt Toto back to him. Surely he can't have gone too far. Luckily for Shaun there were no side roads to make him have to choose which direction to take next. Either side of him there were fields, ahead was one long and winding road.

"Toto, you bastard dog!" He shouted in anger, then changed his tone quickly. Toto would only cower somewhere if he thought Shaun was cross with him. "Treats, Toto. Come and get your treats."

He walked some more and as he turned a corner the wind suddenly gathered strength. It whipped up the sandy soil from the farmland around him. The thick mass whirled and circled his tired body, growing more dense and higher until he could no longer see in front of him. He couldn't see his hands or the pavement. He didn't know where the pavement ended or the road began and he prayed that no cars were coming along the road.

The dust storm was clogging up his eyes and blinding him. He was breathing in the dust through his nose and when he opened his mouth to shout 'Toto' again, the gritty soil filled his mouth and choked him. He reached out to the sides with both of his arms as he walked, hoping to feel the hedge that would serve as a guide. If he could find the hedge he could follow it and it would keep him in, away from the road.

There was a sound to his right. He listened. The wind howled and the trees rustled. He strained to hear the sound again. There it was definitely to his right. It seemed to be a yelp. It was an animal noise and he had heard Toto yelp several times when he had accidentally stood on him. The dog was always getting in the way.

Shaun was sure it was Toto. He turned to the right, still with his arms out to the side. Still no sign or touch of a hedge. He stopped to listen again. Just above the sound of the wind, just very slightly, he could distinguish a dog's howl. Toto must be stuck or hurt. He cursed himself again for leaving the door open on such a dreadful night.

68

"Toto. I'm coming." The wind swallowed up his words immediately they left his mouth.

His eyes were smarting and watering. They had cleared enough for him to make out slight outlines of trees ahead. If this was the wooded area past Carter's farm then he had walked over two miles. Surely not, he hadn't been out that long. He certainly hadn't been walking quickly because the wind had pushed against him at times. It had been hard going. He had been buffeted from all directions, but he couldn't think of where else he would be. There wasn't a wood of any sort for five miles or more, and that was by the sand dunes on the opposite side of the town.

A howl, so close, made him jump. He spun around to the left. As he did so, the dirt from the ground rose up and sprayed his face. He reeled in shock, staggering backwards and landing on his elbow, he lay sprawled on the ground. A sharp pain seared up his arm. With his other hand he tried wiping the grit and sandy soil from his eyes, but he just made it worse. He couldn't see. His eyes burned and his elbow pained.

A voice coming from in front of him made him start.

"D'you need help, mate?"

"Can you help me up? I think I've done my elbow in." Shaun held his good arm out in the general direction of the voice. "Where did you appear from?"

"You're outside my house. I heard you shout. Thought you were Dorothy, mate." The voice laughed.

Shaun feeling, faint with the pain, couldn't think straight.

"Dorothy?"

"Yeah, you shouted Toto. But if you are Dorothy I'm the Wizard of Oz."

Shaun detected a slight note of bitterness in the stranger's voice before he passed out.

When he came to, he felt woozy, still blinded by the dirt and aware that he was no longer outside. He appeared to be lying on a couch. It was warm and he could hear a fire crackling in the hearth. He tried to sit up.

A voice said, "Welcome back to the living."

"How long have I been out for?" asked Shaun, feeling concerned. He still had to look for Toto, and Clare would be worried. She wouldn't know where he was. The thought occurred to him that he didn't know where he was either.

"Several hours. The gales are still raging outside, you won't be going anywhere for a while yet. Would you like a drink?"

Shaun ran his tongue around his dry mouth. He could feel the grit and his throat hurt.

"Please." He said.

"Tea, coffee, whisky?"

"Coffee, thanks, I am so thirsty."

"Aren't you thirsting for alcohol? I can make it a large whisky. Put a fire in your belly."

"Coffee is fine thanks."

"Can I tempt you with some whisky in your coffee? Give it a kick."

"Ok then. Thanks."

"Yes. I thought you could be a man who would be tempted. You like your kicks."

Shaun thought it a strange comment, but his elbow hurt and his brain was fogged and he couldn't be bothered puzzling over throw away comments. Instead he turned his attention to where he might be.

He still couldn't see. His eyes, full of dirt, had swollen and no matter how he tried he couldn't open them. He couldn't remember a house being

70

by the woods. There was Carter's farm, but he knew Robert Carter, they played football together in St Luke's Old Boys. Other than the farm, the only building by the woods was the old chapel. There wasn't a rectory at the chapel, it was serviced by the two vicars from St Luke's and All Saints.

Maybe the trees he saw weren't a wood at all. Perhaps he had just seen a couple of trees and the sandstorm had made it look bigger. He felt uncomfortable. There were three houses along the lane after the chapel. The middle one had three tall trees by the remote control gates. The houses were set back from the road though so how had the guy heard him shout 'Toto' above the sound of the wind? The house with the remote control gates had an intercom. You didn't have to press a button on it to be heard, you only had to beep or shout, it was on all the time. He knew the study to the right of the front door had an open fire. He started to sweat. He tried to calculate the distance walking from his own house to the big house. No, he couldn't have walked that far, it was another mile and a half from the chapel. There were a few sharp turns in the road before then too, and he knew he hadn't made any sharp turns.

The stranger appeared with a hot mug of coffee that smelt strongly of whisky. He helped Shaun up to a sitting position then he took Shaun's hand and placed the handle in it and closed Shaun's fingers around the handle.

"Could I ask you to help me open my eyes...? Sorry, I don't know your name. I'm Shaun." He paused waiting for the stranger to volunteer his name, but when the stranger didn't say anything he carried on. "I could do with washing the grit and dirt out of my eyes. If you have a bowl of water and a towel, I could have a go myself." He tried to make a joke. "You don't have to play at doctors and nurses."

"Do you like playing at doctors and nurses Shaun? Is that how you get your kicks Shaun?"

The stranger was being weird, but unable to see or fend for himself, Shaun was at a disadvantage. He didn't want to anger this man so he bit his tongue and went along with the lame joke. "Not today, mate."

"So I could tempt you another day then, Shaun?"

Shaun squirmed, the conversation was getting weird. He risked annoying the stranger.

"Can you just get me a bowl of water and a towel? Please."

He heard the stranger move away and once more the door opened and closed. There was the sound of running water and doors or drawers being opened and closed and voices. There were voices! Shaun strained to hear. It was a murmur at first but then he heard a woman's voice. It was Eve! He heard Eve's voice, he was sure of it. The stranger would be Eve's husband. He raked through his memory to try to recall Eve's husband's name. As far as he could remember she had only ever called him 'baldy'.

The woman's voice had stopped and he heard footsteps approaching, the door opened and he sensed the stranger standing over him.

"Shaun, my name's Theo. I'm putting the bowl of water on your lap. Don't spill it." Theo placed the bowl of water on Shaun's lap and the towel he placed on Shaun's shoulder.

"Thanks, Theo." Shaun couldn't recall Eve ever calling her husband Theo so he started to relax. He cupped his right hand and scooped some water in to it from the bowl, then he bent his head over his hand with his right eye in the water.

"If you don't get your kicks from doctors and nurses then Shaun, do you get them from other men's wives?"

Shaun sat upright. Had he heard that correctly? "Pardon?"

"Do you get your kicks from having affairs with other men's wives then Shaun?"

Oh God, thought Shaun, this is Eve's husband.

"No! Not at all. Theo. Not at all." He objected. Then added for good measure, "I love my wife."

There was a silence and Shaun took the chance to scoop up more water in his right hand and dip his left eye in it.

"So then, Shaun, you are saying I couldn't tempt you with my wife."

Shaun sat up again, water running down his face, his eyes still swollen and gunged up with dirt. He still couldn't see his tormentor but he didn't care now that he was at a disadvantage. He wasn't taking this sort of grilling from any man.

"For God's sake, man! What the hell do you think you are playing at? D'you get some perverse sense of pleasure from goading a man in pain and distress. I have no intention of betraying my wife."

"Ah, but you do, and have, Shaun Taylor. I am only repeating what has been said. While your wife is preoccupied with caring for your twin babies, you are carrying on with a married woman, who has no children."

"Who said that?" Shaun splashed his eyes with more water and wiped them on the towel. Theo was quiet, so he repeated the process. He could now open his eyes but still couldn't see. Everything was a blur.

Theo changed his attack.

"You could be tempted by a life without babies, couldn't you Shaun? They're nasty crying, troublesome things. They take up all your wife's

73

time and attention and keep her from waiting on your every whim, don't they? She smells of milk vomit, her hair is a mess and she is too tired for sex."

"Shut up!" shouted Shaun. "Shut up. You know nothing. I love those babies. I love my wife. I don't need anything else. Just shut your foul mouth up."

"But Shaun, we both know that's not true, don't we?"

Shaun scrubbed more water over his eyes and rubbed them with the towel.

"You wanted this other woman, you were tempted by her beauty. She didn't have unkempt hair, she smelt of Dior not vomit. She was wealthy and didn't want children. Her career paid too much to give it all up for brats. If you left your wife for her you could have everything your lust desired. She tempted you with promises and like Adam and the apple you believed her. Being a solicitor she could get around the law, she said, and you would come out of it all with the upper hand; quids in, big house with remote control gates, no whinging drab wife, no screaming smelling babies. A woman who loved you, loved sex and earned more than you could ever dream of. Believe me, Shaun Taylor, you were tempted. What stalled you?"

"You're lying! That's not true. I love my wife. Those babies are everything to me. I love their smiling faces, their baby smell. I love that their tiny hands wrap themselves around my fingers. I love that they fix their eyes on my face and follow my every movement, and I love that my wife... that Clare feeds and bathes them so tenderly. Her hair flops down over her eyes as she watches them feed, and because she doesn't have a hand free to push the hair back, I want to go to her and push it back for her and watch the babies suckle, but I don't.

She doesn't need me to help. I would get in her way." The tears ran down Shaun's face and with them the sand and soil, dirt and dust. For the first time in that stranger's house he could see.

He could see the sharp features and the twisted expression on Theo's face. He could see the shame he felt in the air. He could see himself for what he was: selfish. Thinking of just one person, himself, when three other people relied on him. He could see how, by some miracle, he had been stopped wrecking their lives. Relieved that he didn't do as Eve had been begging him. That he hadn't left his wife because he really did love her. As for the twins, he would die for them rather than abandon them.

As if Theo had picked up on his thoughts he waved Shaun's mobile in the air.

"It's all on here." He smirked. "It's not lies. I have the evidence. I'm sure your wife would be interested in your promise to Eve to leave them. All I have to do is press send and the text I have written, that you didn't have the courage to send, will wing its way to your wife. Then you will be free to be with my Eve. That's what you wanted all along, right? You didn't take much tempting."

"Burn in hell!" cried Shaun, launching himself at Theo.

Theo stumbled backwards and fell against the wall. Shaun took his chance and ran towards what he thought was the way out. It was the kitchen. He spun around looking frantically for a door leading outside. There was none. He had no choice but to make a run through the lounge to the other door.

With a heavy heart he made his way home. It was still dark but the wind seemed to have eased slightly.

He had almost lost his wife and twins, he didn't want to risk losing them again

75

The walk home didn't take as long as he thought it would. He found the hedge easily and followed it until he could see his way back.

He opened the door and his wife ran to him.

"Where have you been?" demanded Clare. "I thought you said you would stay in with me tonight. Have you been down to the pub again?"

Shaun put his arm around Clare and pulled her to him. He breathed in the milk posset smell in her tousled hair and kissed the top of her forehead. She looked at him and smiled.

"What's that for?"

"I'm sorry, love. I did an awful thing. I opened the door to see how bad the storm was outside and I let Toto out. I know, I was careless. He ran off and I followed, but I lost him. I've been looking for him. But no success. I'm hoping someone will find him when the storm dies down."

"Toto? You're going to have to do better than that, Shaun. Toto's been curled up on the rug by the Moses baskets all night." She pointed into the lounge. Sure enough, Toto was curled up by the twins. Shaun went over and ruffled his fur. Unlike Shaun, Toto had no dust, sand, grit or evidence of being out in a storm at all. Clare could see that Shaun was genuinely puzzled. She went over to Shaun and put her arms around his waist.

"Maybe he came back in again straight away and you didn't notice."

"That's possible, I suppose." Shaun nodded.

Clare poked him in the arm. He winced.

"You could have phoned, though, to let me know where you where or what you were doing. I could have saved you the trouble and me the worry."

It dawned on Shaun then that Theo still had his phone.

He said nothing to Clare about the house and Theo. He told her he had fallen and it must have fallen out of his pocket then.

Shaun couldn't sleep. At about 3am the wind died down and he carefully got out of bed so as not to wake Clare and took his clothes downstairs to get dressed. He made himself a cup of tea, then silently opened the door to the twins' bedroom. He gently stroked each tiny hand, kissed their foreheads, and sat watching them sleep.

Outside two figures stepped out of the shadows.

"Are you going to give him his phone back?"

"No. I'm going to make him stew."

"I think he's scared enough. He won't do it again."

"Who's next on our list?"

"George Roberts. He's been defrauding his client."

"Do you have a plan, D'evil?"

"Stick to the usual one, Eve. You tempt him and I'll..."

Rough with smooth

He shakes the socks,
At me he glares.
These socks should be in pairs,
He mocks.
I sigh
I wonder why.
No matter how I try,
The socks slip by me.

We Tango weekly.
I don't know why though,
I always quick, when I should slow,
slow, meekly.
I sigh
I wonder why,
No matter how I try,
The steps defy me.

I made him eggs
He wanted runny
They turned out dry and funny.
He gags.
I sigh,
I wonder why.
No matter how I try.
The skill escapes me.

I iron his shirts.
He likes them crease free
But smooth resists me.
It hurts.
I sigh
I wonder why,
No matter how I try.
The iron hates me.

We have a row.
He shakes his socks. Tough.
I won't take smooth with rough,
Not now.
I cry
I wonder why
No matter how I try,
The Gods have left me.

But wait, a fall.
The stairs defeat him.
At the bottom death greets him.
I call
I cry
Then wonder why
I miss him. I sigh.
The quiet bores me.

Defying the odds

Aries: Stay indoors today. Today you will get a visit from the past. To avoid a nasty surprise, don't leave your house.

"What a load of tosh." Marina folded up the newspaper and threw it on the coffee table. Draining her mug of coffee and inhaling the last of her cigarette, she grabbed her handbag and rummaged through it, looking for her car keys.

Not in her bag.

Marina made a habit of leaving her car keys in her bag. She had a last look, emptying out the contents on the coffee tale.

They still weren't there.

"Damn those blasted keys."

She snorted and looked out of the window. The sky was heavy and grey. The wind made a long low whistle through the trees at the corner of the house.

She grabbed her coat.

Something jangled in the pocket and, relieved, she thrust her hand into the gap.

Just her house keys.

Reluctant to leave the warmth of the house, she opened the front door and stood there weighing up her need for cigarettes against the chances of being caught in a downpour.

She needed her cigarettes.

Curling her hand around the house keys, she made her decision and stepped out onto the path, closing the door behind her. Despite the heavy, threatening sky and the strong wind that was tugging and pulling at her and forcing its way into her coat slowing her progress along the pavement, it wasn't as cold as she first thought.

Marina pushed her hood down onto her shoulders. Once her head was uncovered, the many hands and fingers of the wind began attacking her hair. The hair slide was wrenched from her crown and hair tumbled down the front and sides of her face. She grabbed a handful from in front of her eyes and pushed it behind her ears, only to have it snatched back and wrapped around her face like a veil. Again she pushed it aside, and seeing the zebra crossing stepped into the road.

As the wind whipped Marina's hair out of her grasp and into the air, a small speeding white van turned the corner narrowly missing her, but slammed straight into the side of a black cab spinning it around and clipping it into the side of Marina's hip and thigh, before both vehicles came to a halt on the opposite side of the road.

For a while she swayed, but managed to stay upright.

A car horn, loud and insistent, was ringing in her ears. Feeling dazed, she surveyed the scene in front of her.

The black cab and the small white van were entwined like a Yin and Yang symbol. Marina could see only the drivers. Thankfully there were no passengers in the black cab.

The drivers were arguing.

They were standing in the road, oblivious to Marina, concerned only about their vehicles and their livelihood. Arms waving, fists shaking, practically forehead-to-forehead in tension, anger and frustration.

They didn't notice her.

"Are you hurt? Do you need help?"

Marina turned. She grabbed hold of the concerned young man and wouldn't let go. Her face an unhealthy pale grey, was rapidly turning paler.

She saw him hesitate. He looked as if he didn't want to get involved. He glanced over at the drivers still arguing, then at the mangled vehicles and finally at Marina, who had started shaking.

He reached for his phone and dialled 999. He then told Marina, 'What does it matter if I arrive at the hospital later than I intended. Dad is in a coma. He won't notice what time I arrive.'

Marina kept her hold on the young man. The police arrived seconds before the ambulance, and while the paramedics were attending to Marina, the police began to take statements from the drivers. One of the policemen couldn't take his eyes off Marina; he kept looking over his shoulder and staring at her.

The policeman unnerved her.

She tightened her grip on the young man.

"Come with me," she pleaded with him. "You are going to the hospital anyway – you may as well have a lift there."

Marina was ushered into the ambulance.

The police approached the young man. He told them, "This junction is an accident hotspot. My father had his accident here. He was a pedestrian and on his way to see his new granddaughter, my daughter, at the hospital. He sustained head injuries." The man swept his hand around to emphasise the area. The road narrowed very quickly after being a wide junction. "There should be traffic lights rather than a zebra crossing." The young man's temper increased. "My father is in a coma, linked up to a machine that breathes for him. We may have to make the decision to turn off his life support. This road is a death trap."

The police asked questions.

After giving evidence to the police, he clambered aboard the ambulance to sit next to Marina. She turned to thank him but stopped abruptly when her eyes locked with those of the policeman staring at her through the gap in the closing doors.

Unease crept though her.

Someone had left a newspaper behind. It was the same one she had read that morning. Marina opened it at the coffee morning page to re-read her horoscope. Her eyes scanned the columns for Aries, but to her surprise there was no short warning at all, it was just a rambling general account, very similar to all the other signs. She threw the newspaper to the floor, shrank back into the pillow and sat in silence until the ambulance stopped and the doors opened again outside the hospital A&E.

"It doesn't feel broken, probably just bruised." The doctor turned to wash his hands in the small sink in the corner of the cubicle.

Marina sat looking blankly at the wall in front of her. The young man had left her as soon as the paramedics helped her into a wheelchair. He'd muttered his get well wishes then made his exit towards the wards in the main hospital.

The doctor huddled in the corner with the nurse on duty and after a few minutes of whispers and nodding heads, he approached Marina.

"To be certain, I am requesting an X-ray, although I am sure there are no broken bones. I would normally send you home after a routine check, but because of the shock of the impact, and to err on the safe side, we will keep you in overnight for observation."

Marina showed no reaction.

The doctor glanced at the nurse who shrugged and pulled a face. He turned back to stand in front of Marina and bent his knees until his face was level with hers. He had a kindly face. "I am off duty after this shift. I will sign you over to the care of my colleague. Sister Belling will arrange for you to be taken on to ward one, and the night duty doctor will see you tonight, then again tomorrow morning. No doubt you will be discharged after a good night's sleep."

Marina's hands were shaking.

She hadn't had a cigarette since she'd left the house that morning. She felt tired, sick and dazed. There was a tight knot in the pit of her stomach and her throat felt constricted. Something in the way that the policeman had stared at her worried her. They hadn't interviewed her at the scene, instead she heard them tell the paramedic they knew where she lived and would catch up with her later. What did they mean by later? Why did they know where she lived, or did they mean they expected to find her in the hospital?

She wanted to move, but her lifeless legs were pinned to the bed by an invisible force and her shoulders felt leaden and too heavy to lift off the bed.

She shivered.

At the nurses station they were discussing Marina. They had seen previous cases of people shaking as much as Marina was. After an intense debate, they telephoned the doctor on duty for advice.

Minutes later, a nurse was despatched to the pharmacy, returning with a mild sedative. They took Marina's blood pressure and pulse then handed her a glass of water with the tablet.

The doctor visiting her was vaguely familiar. Marina struggled to wake up. Her eyes were heavy and her vision hazy. She tried to ask if she could go home, but her words fell from her lips in a molten heap, each running into the other, making no sense, so she gave up.

Rahas, the doctor, bent over her and shone a small torch in her eyes, lifting her eyelids up one at a time to do so. He was so close to her face that she could feel his breath on her skin.

The breath was icy.

Marina's pulse quickened, her skin paled, beads of sweat collected on her forehead, her whole body became clammy, and fear crept slowly and painfully up from her feet. She made to speak again but although her lips moved, no sound escaped. The doctor moved closer until he became a blur in front of Marina's eyes. His icy lips brushed her ear and he lowered his voice. "You shouldn't be in here. You threw away your chance. You had been warned." He moved away, leaving Marina chilled.

The evening crept into the night. Marina alternated between waves of fear-induced nausea and drug-induced sleep. She tossed and thrashed about, suffocating with night terrors. They started as the regular bad dreams she experienced at home, when the doctor, whom she soon realised was the protagonist in her original bad dreams, was holding her close and breathing poisonous gas into her mouth. At one point she awoke from the depths of a nightmare, only to find herself being pulled back down in to it, the doctor grasping her again by the neck and clamping his mouth over hers.

She gasped for air.

At the bottom of her bed, the nurse was talking in hushed tones to the doctor. Marina drifted in and out of consciousness. She wanted to listen to what they were saying but the effort of concentrating made her feel nauseous and drained her of energy. She was drowsy. It was easier for her to give in to sleep than fight it.

Marina opened her eyes.

The nurse and doctor had disappeared. Walking towards her was the young man she clung to in the road. He stopped at her bed.

"I'm on my way to visit my dad and thought I'd look in on you. I asked at A&E how you were and they said they'd kept you in." Marina didn't reply. He shuffled awkwardly on the spot. He had his baby with him. "I've brought my daughter in for my dad, though of course, I know he can't see her, but I hope he will sense her."

The young man moved closer to Marina, holding out the baby. The baby cried out loud and didn't stop screaming until she was moved away from Marina. Feeling flustered, the man made his excuses and left. The baby calmed down...

Marina made no sound.

She had neither acknowledged the young man nor noticed the baby. She felt sick. Every time she awoke she felt worse. Her limbs ached and burned from the sensation of thousands of hot needles pricking her skin.

When Marina next awoke she had a tube in her arm. Her eyes wouldn't open enough to see properly, but she could just about make out the shape of a drip stand and bag. She felt a frisson of unease. Marina sensed rather than noticed the police enter the ward. They were accompanied by a nurse.

Marina slipped into sleep.

"What's wrong with her?" One of the policeman bent down and peered into Marina's face.

"Shock mainly," replied the nurse, "although she is a bit of a puzzle. We can't find any other reason for her rapid withdrawal. She wasn't seriously hurt in the accident. Just bruised."

"It was almost on the spot where she had her car incident months before..." One of the policemen – the one who had stared at Marina – suddenly announced where he had seen her previously.

The sergeant glanced at him and raised his eyebrows.

"She caused an accident by driving her car erratically and at speed. I'd swear she'd been drinking, sergeant, but she tested negative for alcohol. She pleaded that her foot had slipped off the brake on to the accelerator when a cat had run out in front of her car, sending her careering out of control."

"What has that to do with her being the victim in this incident?"

"Nothing really, I suppose I find it strange... As if I'm missing something. Like a piece of jigsaw that doesn't fit, but should." He stared at Marina.

The sergeant then turned to the nurse and gave instructions to be notified when Marina was feeling able to communicate. They left, but as they went, Marina managed to open an eye, only to catch the policeman staring back at her. He made a slight motion of running his finger across his throat, although his facial expression didn't change.

The shaking started again.

Three nurses ran to her bedside and busied themselves, checking her drip, blood pressure, temperature and pulse. Marina was sweating, but her body was clammy and cold. Her skin had a greyish translucent pallor and her eyes appeared too small in her sockets. The nurses held a hushed discussion at the foot of her bed, glancing over occasionally at Marina.

The doctor was called.

He stood by her bed. A figure in black, dark

hair, dark beard, black clothes. Marina tried to open her eyes wider but the fluorescent light shining behind his head blinded her already sensitive and sore eyes, so she closed them again.

As the doctor moved closer, her body tensed. The shaking became jerking convulsions and the sweat ran from her brow. He held his hand out to the nurse and she filled a syringe from a phial and handed it to him. He leant over Marina and whispered in her ear. "You'd been taking drugs and the police missed that didn't they? You went straight to your car after doing cocaine and drove straight into the pedestrian." His breath icy against her ear sent her into more convulsions as fear gripped her heart and throat. "The innocent gentleman you mowed down is going to have his life support switched off tomorrow. The police may have missed the evidence but we didn't. You can't run, no one can. Your sins will always find you out."

He injected the sedative.

Hallucinations plagued her day, and the night terrors increased. Marina fought to wake, but a group of hooded figures dressed in black, dark facial hair covering their features, pulled her back into the horrors of her subconscious. In the darkest area of the pit she was surrounded by floating black semi-transparent birds or devilish creatures, at first swooping down at her then circling her at speed snapping at her face and brushing past her. In her nightmare she ran towards a gap. In her bed she was thrashing about, grasping and grappling with the bed covers as the faceless beings chased and grazed her.

She managed to open her eyes.

She was really awake.

For the first time in two days she could see

clearly the beds, the curtains, other patients asleep, and at the top of the ward she could see the nurses' station. She opened her mouth to shout for help. As she did so a black figure appeared from behind the bed frame, and clamping his mouth over hers, breathed in. Marina was pinned to the bed, unable to move, unable to breathe, and the figure continue to suck in the air from her lungs. Clamped onto her lips until it was satisfied it had sucked her last breath, the figure then evaporated into the air and disappeared.

Marina lay there lifeless.

Sounds from an alarm startled the young man. He heard a gasp. He looked down at his daughter who had ceased her cries and was gurgling happily. Realising that something else was different, he turned to see his father lying in the bed with his eyes open and smiling at his new granddaughter.

In his office, Dr Rahas Khama checked his list of patients for the day. He crossed off one and marked a tick against the other. He placed his notes and the files in his case, cleared his desk and left the office, locking the door behind him.

His job was done.

A Greek Tragedy

Inspired by a hole in a garden wall

My love for you is this: a shiny blade
That pierces skin and kills the bloody soul,
Then drains a bright life, makes a sweet breath
fade.
For once a life is snuffed, it leaves a role

That no other can creep to take its place.
Dead sweet lover, this deed as black as coal
Has robbed me, of love, ripped a gaping space
In my heart. What is left of pacts we made?
Can fate now split us? End here, all a waste?

Think not! Through a wall our love has been
played,
Whispered sweet nothings through a crack for
years
Planned to elope, but hopes in this spot fade
When a lioness gave your Thisbe fears
I ran, you found my shawl soiled, ripped apart.

Then through your tragic grief and forlorn tears,
Your sword, you drove, through your poor
wretched heart.
Now shall this blade, my love, bind you with me.
On this spot, in the next life we will start Anew.
Pyramus and his love Thisbe.

A Terza Rima

Wicked words and dastardly deeds

"So, what are you going to do then Soph?"

Natalie pushed away her cappuccino cup, sat back, and looked directly at her sister.

"Every time we meet for lunch or a coffee, all you do is moan about him. Moan, moan, complain and more moan. Moaning about him isn't going to solve anything. You need to do something or put up with it."

"It's alright for you, Nat. You and Lee have it all sorted. He works away and you live in that big posh house and spend all his money. You have it all, and that's what I want too. It's not a lot to ask. Is it?

"You'll have it all one day, Soph. You just have to be patient."

"Is that meant to be a joke? Patient? When he was my patient he was at death's door. The consultant told us many times he shouldn't be alive, that it was a miracle he survived. It was my nursing that kept him going, he said. That's why Gerald married me, I suppose. So he had someone to care for him. I was just blinded by all his wealth and his laddish smile. I've had my fill of patients and patience."

"Who are you trying to kid? You made a play for him when you knew he was a lawyer and loaded. I bet you practically shoved your chest into his face every time you tucked him in his hospital bed."

Sophie pushed out her chest and moved her shoulders backwards and forwards and they both laughed.

"Seriously, Nat. I need out, but if I divorce him I get nothing," she said as they stood up to leave the cafe.

"Are you sure he has got it all tightly sewn up?" Nat asked once they were outside.

"Definitely. He showed me the documents before they were left at the solicitor's office. I couldn't object without looking as though I was only marrying him for his money."

"You were."

Sophie frowned.

"I didn't think he'd last for years after the op. The consultant told the ward staff that it would probably tide him over for six months to a year at the most. So when Gerald said that he was adding a clause were I was only entitled to a pay out if he divorced me or on his death, I saw no reason to object. I could tell him I wasn't after his money, and look as though I meant it."

"And all you had to do was sit back and wait for the months to pass."

"Only it's been four Godawful years." Sophie grabbed her sister's arm. "And I've had enough, but I'm not leaving him without being paid for my suffering."

"Suffering?"

"He knew I hated nursing. I told him often enough. It got me down going to work every day on a ward full of whinging patients. Listening to all their ailments, demands for bed pans and for their sheets to be straightened." She mimicked them. "Can you just make me comfy, nurse? Can you pass me my drink, nurse? Could you fill my water jug, nurse? "She scrunched her face into a mock pleading look. "I was just a bloomin' skivvy! He promised me I could pack my job in at the hospital when we were married."

"Which you did..."

"Which I did. Then he packed in his job at the law firm and went to work for charities giving free advice to the elderly, disabled and disadvantaged! Then he only goes and volunteers me to work in a crummy old people's care home for half the wage I was getting at the hospital. If I stay any longer, he will have given all his money to the charities, and I'll be worse off than I was before I met him."

They stopped outside a bookstore while Sophie rummaged in her handbag for a tissue. She found one, blew her nose, and wiped her eyes.

"Crumbs, Soph, I thought you were a toughie. Must be bad if he's driven you to tears."

"Gerald couldn't drive a mouse out of a nest. I'm angry, Nat. I'm angry because he's loved by everyone. I'm angry because he will do anything for anyone. These are tears of anger, Nat, because he is so giving to everyone that there will be nothing left for me except a poorly paid job."

"A poorly paid job which he presumes you took on willingly because you loved him and he told everyone at the time that you shared his passion for helping others, too!"

"Because I thought he only had six months left to live. I told him I shared the same interest because I didn't think I'd be... Nat are you listening to me?"

Natalie had half turned from Sophie and was staring in the shop window.

"Wait here," she ordered.

Sophie fumed. When she was in full rant, she expected her sister to listen to her. She was ready to give her a piece of her mind when Natalie came out of the shop, but stopped at the sight of her smiling and waving a paper bag, saying gleefully, "Your troubles are over, Soph. In my hand I hold your future."

Sophie grabbed the bag and pulled out a small book.

"An A-Z of plants that kill, paralyse, maim and intoxicate! Are you out of your mind, Nat? The first thing they would do at a postmortem is look for anything suspicious in the blood or body. I'd be rumbled straight away."

"I've already flicked through it. There are ordinary garden plants whose parts can bring on a heart attack. No one would suspect a man with a dicky heart, who is living on borrowed time, dying from a heart attack. I doubt they would hold a postmortem in his case."

Sophie's eyes lit up and a slow smile crept across her face as she mulled over the idea in her mind. Eventually she spoke.

"Nat, you're a genius." She gave her sister a hug. "Come on, let's discuss the plan over some lunch."

The sisters walked down the road into the town centre. Sophie splashed out on some trendy designer clothes from her meagre wage. She chose a black dress and jacket and some four-inch heeled court shoes to match. She didn't even tell her sister that she chose them with Gerald's funeral in mind. She'd convinced herself that she needed to look smart, as was befitting her status as a lawyer's wife.

They chose to eat at the trendy wine bar on Southwark Street. It was the place that Gerald had taken her to on their first date, and where he had proposed to her on their third date. How fitting that she should plan his demise there. It would be the last time she ate there as Gerald's wife. The thought sent a tingle down her spine. She cast a quick look around as they chose their table just to make sure that Gerald wasn't in there, too. Then they made their order from the menu before getting the book out to flick through it.

"Here, Soph, the root of monkshood looks like horseradish but is poisonous and the seeds of the yew berry are poisonous as are the leaves. All you need are a few seeds sprinkled in his muesli at breakfast, or added to a dressing for his salads."

"You're joking aren't you? Muesli? Gerald won't

94

touch the stuff. Rabbit food he calls it." She took a swig of her wine and deepened her voice to imitate her husband. "Nothing like a good cooked English breakfast to set you up of a morning, Sophie. You need feeding up. You're too thin, dear. No substance in those meals. If God had meant you to eat dried oats and lettuce, he would have given you long ears and whiskers. Slap another rasher in that pan, will you, dear"

Natalie was laughing.

"It's not funny. I'm sick of hearing it. I try adding extra fat and butter at every opportunity as well, because it's obviously the clogged arteries from all the fried rich fatty foods that led to his heart attack in the first place but he is still around."

"Then it will have to be the monkshood root in the horseradish sauce with a hearty roast dinner."

"Roll on Sunday." chuckled Sophie and, raising her glass, added; "Here's to singledom!"

They clinked glasses just as Natalie noticed Gerald and a taller, suited gentleman leave the wine bar and step into the street. Sophie followed her gaze.

"Oh crikey," she said, "Where was he sitting?"

Nat shook her head. "He can't have been near or we'd have seen him, wouldn't we?"

They watched him walk off without a backwards glance. If Gerald had seen or heard them, he made no signs of it.

Sophie breathed a sigh of relief, finished her glass of wine, and poured herself another from the bottle.

It was late when the sisters finally left the wine bar and even later when Sophie opened the door to a dark and empty house. It wasn't unusual for Gerald to go out in an evening and, as she only had herself to cater for, she couldn't be bothered cooking. After looking in the fridge and cupboards, she settled for a pot of yoghurt. She went through to the study and picked up her lap top to take back into the kitchen. While she waited for the lap top to boot up, she sprinkled some nuts and the last of the muesli on to the yoghurt, poured herself yet another glass of wine from the fridge, and sat down to google for places to find or buy monkshood.

Just after midnight, Gerald opened the door to the kitchen to put the kettle on and was shocked to see Sophie slumped over her lap top. He had expected her to be in bed. He cried out, and his friend who was in the lounge came running. Seeing Gerald's wife lying there he made a quick examination. As he moved her slightly to feel for a pulse, the screen glowed and the page she had been studying opened. He read the screen, released Sophie slowly and pulled his phone out of his jacket pocket.

"Hello, Sarge. I may have found a suicide. Can you get the team out to me? No, I'll leave it till they arrive. I can't deal with it. I've been drinking all evening with the deceased's husband at the police charity event. Thanks."

"I need some air." Gerald felt sick.

"You look whiter than pale, Ged. What a shock for you. I'll make the coffee while you step outside for a few minutes."

Shaking, Gerald left the house by the back door. He picked up a tissue from behind the plant pot and shook the contents down the grid. Then he returned inside and went straight to the downstairs toilet where he flushed the tissue away. He thought of Sophie and her hateful shrill voice in the wine bar saying how poisonous yew berry seeds were.

What a blessing that Sophie had chosen to eat

the muesli for supper instead of breakfast. She had unwittingly provided him with the most convincing alibi.

Going Boldly on Bold Street

Going boldly on Bold Street.
Having a lark on Lark Lane,
Feeling the spirit in Church Street,
Lord Street I feel like a Dame.

On Hope Street Cathedrals uplift me.
In Lime Street the traveller returns.
Two tunnels to cross the Mersey,
Ferry back to our great Liver Birds.

Dodgy Business

I was enjoying a very good quality wine in the lounge, looking out at the Formby dunes through the large windows and relaxing after a long day at work, when I spied a movement in the garden. I craned my neck to see properly.

Whatever it was had moved out of sight.

I wondered if it could have been a fox, as the shrubs in that area of the garden were only a few feet high. I was about to get out of my seat and wander over to the window for a better look when Alan came through the door, followed by his wife.

For some unknown reason, instead of carrying on towards the window, I quickly sat back down again. I caught Alan and his wife exchange a look. Although nothing was mentioned, I imagined they thought they had caught me being nosey or snooping around their lounge.

No longer relaxed, I dismissed the urge to explain myself and instead commented on the wine. As I did so, I realised my boss might think I was about to help myself from the bottle he'd left on the side table.

His raised eyebrows confirmed it and, to my embarrassment, he strode over, picked up the bottle, and made to fill my glass.

"No, no." I put my hand over the glass, "I don't want anymore. I have to drive home."

Instead, he introduced me to Maria.

I stood up to shake her hand. As I put my hand out towards her, I caught sight of another movement outside, this time a bit nearer.

"Gerri!"

I was still standing with my hand out towards Maria, but hadn't got around to shaking her hand.

"I'm sorry, Maria, I thought I saw a—" I shook my head to erase the image and indicate that my

99

attention was back in the room. As I shook her hand, she appeared to tense.

I couldn't explain what I thought I had just seen in their garden, so I babbled instead.

"This wine is strong!" I looked at the glass. "It has me seeing things."

Alan was obviously irritated with me. He drew a sharp intake of breath, opened his mouth to speak, but closed it before the words could escape. Maria shot me a sideways glance and then glared at him.

It was all my fault. Alan had been laughing and joking on the way home. I had watched him, in admiration, at the meeting. He secured a massive contract for the company, which would guarantee safe jobs for the work force for years to come. I don't know how he did it, but he appeared to know just what they were thinking, and there were fourteen people around the table. He delivered his proposal then went on to cover each area from all the rival firms, so that when it was their turn to deliver, they had nothing new to offer.

If I didn't know better, I would say that he had read all their papers before lunch and altered his talk to take in all the extra points.

I was about to praise him, and tell Maria what a top boss he was when I had the uneasy feeling of being watched. I turned quickly and caught sight of a pair of eyes under a wide hat, staring in through the window.

I jumped up and pointed.

"There's someone looking in at the window!"

To my surprise, Alan and Maria didn't move. They didn't seem anxious or concerned. I queried it.

"Gerri, dear, this house is enormous. If I were to run out of the side door to take chase, they would be out of sight before I cornered the house."

Alan patted my shoulder. "After a long day in a very long meeting, I could do without the exercise. They will be long gone now."

"Long gone." Maria repeated it more firmly for my benefit. A fleeting suspicion that she was warning me off, crossed my mind.

"Oh well, if you're sure..." I tried to make my voice sound light. "Can I use your loo?"

Once more they exchanged looks before Maria gave me the directions.

I started to feel uneasy – and even more so when Alan stood by the lounge door watching me walk down the hall to the bathroom. Maybe he thought I was going to look for their wine cellar.

When I opened the bathroom door, I came face to face with the intruder.

I screamed.

"What on earth? Who are you?" I demanded.

Alan rushed over and steered me away as the intruder ran for the door.

Maria sat in the chair wringing her hands.

Alan paced the floor, rubbing his chin and head alternately.

I reached for the wine, without waiting to be asked, and poured myself a full glass. If there was a right moment to become an alcoholic, this was it. I had just witnessed the strangest sight. I couldn't believe what my eyes had just seen.

I waited for the explanation. It was a long time coming, and when it did, it started with an unexpected question.

"Do you have Irish heritage, Gerri?"

"My Grandmother was Irish."

"That will explain it." Alan nodded to Maria who sank back in her chair. She had the look of a woman, who had just been told she had a wrong number on her lottery ticket, after she had spent thousands celebrating.

"We know the intruder, Gerri. No one but yourself has seen him here. I think you only saw him because you have some sort of similar Irish heritage. It can be the only explanation. That's how we can see him, it appears."

"Who is he? Why do you let him wander around your house and grounds? Why have you never mentioned him? Oh God! How old is he?"

Alan moved to the arm of the chair where Maria sat, and placed his hand on his wife's shoulder.

"It's not what I suspect you think."

It dawned on me that I had missed part of the conversation, in my light-headed, shocked state.

"What do you mean, I only saw him because of my Irish heritage?"

"I'll start from the beginning." said Alan. 'It's okay Maria, I trust Gerri. If I didn't have Kenny to do the work, I would have to ask Gerri."

I noticed him stroke Maria's cheek before resting his hand back on her shoulder.

"Maria likes to stroll along the dunes and beach on fine days. She has often found items lost by others who may have walked there too. Sometimes she finds things amongst the waste that have been washed ashore from ships. Our lives changed one day when she had the most amazing find - a body in a barrel, washed up on Formby beach. She saw the barrel first, of course, but when she rolled it around to see what it contained, she found the catch to open it, and looked inside. Imagine her shock when she found a lifeless body in it. He had been in there for days, and the barrel reeked of whiskey."

"I thought he was dead." Maria crossed herself. "I tried to phone the ambulance, but I didn't have a signal. So I carried him to the rangers' hut for them to phone someone— but as I was explaining, they looked at me as though I was mad or a hoaxer."

Alan continued. "They couldn't see him. They couldn't understand Maria either. It was as if she was speaking a different language. They shrugged and walked away, leaving her with no choice than to take him to the hospital herself. It was a long walk to the car and he was a dead weight. When she got him to the hospital, they accused her of time wasting. They couldn't see him either. She brought him home and eventually he came out of his unconscious state. He reckons we must be connected to his family, some way back in our history. Apparently they weren't always invisible."

I was too stunned to reply for a while, but when it sank in, I had more questions.

"Why was he in the barrel? Who is Kenny?"

"*He* is Kenny. He looks childlike but assures us he is over seventy years old. He had been stealing whiskey from an inn. They saw him, caught him, locked him in the barrel, and tossed him off the harbour wall. They expected him to drown. Pixies are bad luck, especially thieving pixies. He took the opportunity to drink all the whiskey then passed out. He was lucky that the current from the Irish Sea brought him straight across the bay."

I downed the rest of my glass.

If I hadn't seen the two foot high man for myself, I would think my boss was deranged. I looked at the glass for an answer.

"Did you not wonder how I knew, all the rivals' proposal plans? Kenny makes a good spy. He works for whiskey and lodging. Business has prospered since he arrived. No one else can see him, except you. Which gives me a problem."

"I won't tell anyone. I'm glad the business is doing well. I suppose I feel a bit miffed that you didn't trust me enough to let me in on your..." I paused searching for the right word, "...your secret."

Maria pushed Alan off the arm of the chair and sat up straight. Alan walked to the window and glanced outside. He turned back towards me.

"But now we have told you, we will have to kill you."

Maria moved to the door.

I gripped the chair.

My heart pounded loudly in my ears.

They laughed. A strange sound, not unlike the pantomime villain.

"Only joking!" Alan said.

I sighed with relief.

Maria sneered and blocked the door as Alan started walking towards me, his face painted with a menacing expression and twisting a tie between both hands.

Bradley's Reward

An illustration on an old postcard, of an elderly woman bending over a boy by a river, prompted this piece.

Bradley rued the day he rescued the wizened old woman from the river.

Undecided whether to save her, he had first called, "Why should I get cold and wet rescuing you? Do I get a reward?"

After she had immediately promised him a reward, he'd stripped down to his underwear and jumped in.

Back on the riverbank, Bradley dressed himself, leaving the old woman shivering in her saturated clothes.

"So, what is my reward?" He pulled on his jumper. "It had better be worth it."

The old woman thought for a while, then she swayed and with half-shut eyes, she tilted her chin upwards and croaked her instructions.

Bradley crouched behind the wall.

As the old woman had predicted the five sheep wandered down the hillside to graze beside the gate.

He waited until the full moon was overhead, and picked out the best looking of the five, crept towards it, and tied his rope around the startled sheep.

That turned out to be the easiest bit. The sheep refused to be led to his car, pulling, tugging and bleating loudly, she resisted. Bradley finally opened the boot and lifting up the exhausted sheep, threw her in.

That was when he heard the voices, and caught in the spotlight of police torches, recognised the farmer.

He sat in the dock, as character witnesses told the jury of his bullying ways. They described his persecution of the very elderly in the village, accusing them of being descendants of the Pendle Witches, often vandalising their gardens and writing obscenities on their walls.

Bradley could see the jury absorbing this information. He imagined them seeing it as entertainment. What did they know? They weren't from his village.

He was called to the stand and swore to tell the truth.

"That witch told me to catch the sheep I fancied," he pointed at the old woman, "take it to the river and make it drink from the section of water that shone silver from the light of the full moon. After that the sheep would poo gold coins whenever she saw me."

Shrieks of laughter escaped from the court room.

A Creative Culture
A Villanelle

A changing work of art on the skyline, when
you're leaving
Along a street called Hope, two Cathedrals to call
our own.
If I can't create in Liverpool, why am I breathing?

On a bench, a bronze of Eleanor Rigby sits
dreaming
Life moves on, new talent, fresh breath, creates
alongside old.
A changing work of art on the skyline, when
you're leaving.

Two football teams, red and blue, keep thousands
believing,
Sing, you're in my heart and soul, and you'll never
walk alone,
If I can't create in Liverpool, why am I breathing?

Pioneers, Hornby, Ellis, Hughes, Ross and more,
did the leading,
Willie Russell, and Alan Bleasedale, make
theatres our own.
A changing work of art on the skyline, when
you're leaving.

Humour, Lambananas, a vibrant, city heart
beating.
Ken Dodd and Bessie Braddock share a joke
'neath Lime Street's dome,
If I can't create in Liverpool, why am I breathing?

We have old life to tell the tales, new life to stop it
grieving,

Talented Waterhouse, actors, Baker, Catterall all home grown
A changing work of art on the skyline, when you are leaving
If I can't create in Liverpool, why am I breathing?

A Special Delivery

The postman, a large harassed-looking man dressed in thick jumper and luminous oversized red jacket, knocked at the door. Streams of rain water droplets trickled down his face from his forehead and temple and dripped off his chin and nose.

I had watched him from my spot at the breakfast bar as he tried to cram a package in the letter box, gave up when it wouldn't go through, and tried to yank it out again. The result was a torn padded envelope.

When I opened the door to him he was carrying a bag the size of a small house on his shoulder, and was rummaging through it and muttering.

"Thanks," I said, holding out my hand for the package.

He waved it around in my general direction with his left hand whilst still rummaging in his bag with his right.

"Muh," he said to the ground.

"Pardon?"

"The's muh." he said.

I gave up trying to catch hold of the waving package and waited to see what or how much 'muh' there was.

He grunted and let the bag slide slowly from his shoulder. I half expected him to say *fee fo fi fum* as he bent right down to disembowel the contents of the small house. He slung the original package to the ground, neatly taking off the top of two daffodils which had struggled through the last few weeks of snow and freezing spring conditions to tentatively peep out in full golden glory yesterday afternoon. I scooped them up lovingly and rested them gently on the palm of my hand. Their yellow gold heads, so dainty, looked up at me. Each only had a short length of stalk, but I could put them in an egg cup of water on the window sill. Their struggles wouldn't be in vain and they could still cheer me inside the house.

As I stood looking at these little miracles of nature, the postman let out a triumphant grunt, something akin to a chicken laying an ostrich egg, and slapped with some force a bundle of letters and a larger package onto my outstretched palm—flattening the daffodils.

"There," he grunted, a bit of spit landed on the door frame next to me.

"'Am off! Cheerio." He spun around quite sharply for his large frame and a droplet of sweat dripped off his nose and sailed through the air, narrowly missing my cheek.

I watched him lumber up the drive, closed the door, and took the post through to the kitchen. After making an attempt to pull the daffodil petals back into some sort of shape, I placed them in an egg cup of water, but they drooped dejectedly over the sides. I now had my doubts about their ability to add some cheer to the inside of the house.

I pushed aside the empty breakfast dishes and sat down to investigate my packages.

First I looked at the torn package on the table then at the much larger package and two A4 sized letters which had in large red letters across the front: *Photographs, Do Not Bend.* Why did the postie try cramming the smallest package through the letter box when the rest of the post was much larger? How did he think he would get the rest of the post through? Why didn't he just knock in the first place?

The postmark of one of the A4 envelopes was South Wales, the other was Sheffield. I pushed the Sheffield envelope to one side, since I knew that would contain a picture I had ordered off a

110

printmaker. I tore open the South Wales envelope. It was a large photo of my aunt and her next door neighbour, taken outside the neighbours' front door about... How long ago? Must be twenty five years, at least. I tried to remember when I took the picture.

I was working in Cardiff and needed somewhere to stay. Being part-time and on low pay, I asked my uncle if he knew of anywhere cheap and cheerful in the area. He suggested I stay with them so long as I ignored the rubble and chaos while they renovated their cottage. I had a great week, definitely cheap and extremely cheerful. I had never enjoyed a business trip so much.

Their next door neighbour was a colourful character, and her cats, all six of them, joined us on picnics, jaunts in the forest, and strolls along the coast. She kept them on leads when we were out but in her house they ruled the roost. In the photograph, taken on my last day, she was cradling one cat, whilst two sat on her shoulders and one of her cats swung from the bottom of my auntie's skirt. It made an odd picture and I laughed.

It was the second time that week that I'd seen the picture. My aunt had written to me by email. It was a pleasant surprise but unfortunately, along with a link to the picture, she had written in her native tongue and my Welsh language skills were sketchy. With the help of google translate and the dregs of my memory, I deciphered her letter.

Her neighbour had gone in a home, had left my aunt a cat, and my aunt was looking for a loving home for it. My aunt thought of me because I had met the neighbour twenty years ago. She asked if I would like it. She said it had no tail, probably a Manx cat.

Being a sucker for a sad story I agreed. "How will I get it from you?" I wrote back, since I lived in Yorkshire and didn't have plans for travelling so far south.

I didn't hear any more until this envelope arrived. I looked in the envelope to see if she had sent a note to say they were travelling up to visit their daughter and would drop it in. There was a note but all it said was, "Thought you might like this photo, as it is where the cat came from."

I made a mental note to send her an email and turned to the largest package. Bulky but flattish, it wasn't heavy, but neither was it light. It was like playing a game of *What am I?* I shook it but there was no sound. Eventually I opened it from the end with the least sticky tape, and tipped the contents onto the table.

What I found inside was totally unexpected.

I sat down and tried to decipher the note. The Welsh and the scrawling loopy handwriting made it difficult. All the time I was trying to make sense of the note, the cat's eyes were staring at me, his expression one of horror or shock. His back was arched and his stiff legs were stretched out as if to resist his fate.

I concentrated on the note. As I recognised a word I jotted it down to help me string the sentence together.

I looked at the resulting translation in front of me, then at the photograph with the cats, and then at the cat in front of me.

Yes, that was definitely the cat.

I re-read the note.

"I hope you like the cat, and I am so glad it has found a loving home after spending over twenty years in a drawer, poor thing!"

I opened my iPad and emailed my aunty.

'It is lovely! Thank you.'

After all these years, my aunt had remembered that I had admired the door knocker!

After several hours of hunting, I found some decent screws and a screwdriver and fixed the cat knocker to my front door.

The cat still wore an expression of shock, but the overall effect of a door knocker on my plain old door was a vast improvement.

As the light faded and the night sky was making an appearance, I heard the beating of rain on the window. Glad of the warmth from the fire, I snuggled down on the settee under a furry throw, to read a book. The beating rain grew louder, until it seemed to be knocking at the windows and doors.

It took me a while to realise that the noise actually was a knocking at the door! Fancy forgetting the new door knocker.

I shoved the throw to one side and went into the hall. The temperature difference between the two rooms hit me, and I shivered as I was wrapped in the icy breath from the draughts seeping through the front door and side windows.

The knocking at the door became more persistent.

I wrestled with the door chain, before finally swinging it open.

"Hello?" I called out and, as there was no one in front of me. I stepped out on to the path to get a clearer view, just in case they had taken shelter at the side of the house out of the cutting wind.

I didn't wait long. I was in a flimsy top and the cold was biting into my arms and bare legs. I turned to go back into the house, when a noise brought me to a halt.

I looked at the door, then looked down into the hall.

As the bile rose, I swallowed hard.

The hissing was aggressive, and fear stopped me from moving forward.

The door knocker had disappeared.

On the carpet at the door was the cat, eyes staring at me, his expression of horror replaced by a menacing fury. His back was arched and his stiff legs were stretched as if to pounce should I approach.

I stepped back and as I did so, the door shut, locking me outside.

Turn around Toxteth

*I wrote this in the May when I saw a report on
BBC News that Granby 4 Streets had entered the
Turner Prize. Toxteth won the prize in
December!*

The shortlist is out, for this year's Turner Prize.
On it, jaw dropping news, what a surprise!
A street in Toxteth that was facing demolition
Is among the entries for Turner nomination.

Turn around Turner, the idea's simply a dream
Combination of residents, working as a team.
The owners, some bought their homes for a
pound,
Liked the proposal, and thought it dead sound.

Plans were drawn up, designs set in motion,
Houses stripped out for, creation, renovation.
Forget Emin, the only beds seen on this street
Are bushes, flowers (no weed), all made very
neat.

For twenty years it's been empty. A neglected L8.
If Cairns Street wins, well, that would be great.
So Scousers everywhere, please raise your
glasses.
Here's to Toxteth: rising like a Phoenix from
Ashes.

May the prestigious prize start with a pound
house.
And the best Turner entry, turn out to be Scouse.

A Cloud of Doubt

"A dead body? You've made an appointment for me with the morgue?"

The news sent a shiver running through me.

"Why me? I've never seen a dead body before. Can't you send someone else? There were enough of us there at the time." I held the phone away from my ear and looked at it in disbelief. I could still hear the voice at the other end so I asked her to repeat herself even though I knew I had heard correctly the first time.

"I'm not sure that you've got the right person..."

The voice was adamant and authoritative, and she made it difficult to refuse. The word 'duty' was used several times and, because I had been caught off-guard, I couldn't find the right words to convincingly point her in the direction of someone else. Her decision was final and I was required to turn up on Friday morning at 10am sharp.

"Yes, okay. I'll be there."

When she rang off, I stood for a while with the phone still in my hand. I was shocked, stunned even. Why me, why out of everyone who was at the Village Hall the previous evening, did she single me out?

It was 2 o'clock on a Thursday afternoon. I had answered the phone whilst in the middle of making pastry. My white greased and floury finger prints were all over the telephone receiver. I made to wipe them off with my apron, when I realised that I did not have my apron on. In my haste to answer the phone I had, in fact, wiped my hands down my pleated skirt instead.

I rushed upstairs to divest myself of the floured, greasy skirt, folded it neatly in to a bag to take to the dry cleaners, and replaced it with my cashmere pencil skirt.

I couldn't imagine what a dead body looked like. I have never watched murder mysteries or war programmes on TV so I couldn't even draw on the screen images for an example.

I sat down dejectedly at the dressing table and caught sight, in the mirror, of some smudged mascara on my eyelid.

I leant forward to stare at my reflection. I looked paler than usual, but after that phone call it was not surprising. I made a closer inspection and found myself wondering if the corpse would look white or a greyish white or yellowish grey, or blue tinged. Would his eyes be open and staring or closed? Would he smell of disinfectant or chemicals? If he'd been dirty, would they have washed him completely clean? What would he be wearing?

I closed my eyes and tried a number of facial movements until I settled on one that I imagined would be the right sort of expression for a deceased. I opened one eye to look at the effect but it was so comical that I stood up and moved over to adjust the bedding.

As I plumped up the pillows, I reflected yet again on the deceased.

Would he look like Richard did when he was asleep? He's always dead to the world once his eyes close and his mouth opens, though I know a corpse would be deathly silent and not emit sounds that imitate an avalanche in the Rockies.

From the quick description over the phone he sounded as though he were some sort of vagrant. Dirty, she had said, and with several days' worth of stubble on his face. I conjured up a picture of a greasy-haired tramp with bad breath, and shuddered. The thought made me feel nauseous.

Under different circumstances, it wasn't something I'd have dwelt on for long but since

117

receiving the phone call I could think of nothing else.

I picked up a pile of ironed boxer shorts off the foot of the bed and put them away neatly in Richard's bedside cabinet. As I did so, I knocked his stack of collectible Second World War magazines and they slid to the floor. I started picking them up to put them back, when my imagination got the better of me and I realised that they may hold some clues as to what sort of image one would expect to encounter at the morgue.

I flicked through one magazine then another until I was avidly scouring all of Richard's collection, looking for anything vaguely resembling a dead body.

I suppose a visit to the morgue would put me out of my misery. At least then I'd know what he looked like. Why couldn't it have been a woman, complete with make-up and manicured nails? That would have made things so much easier. I looked at my own immaculate nails, knowing I could relate to a person with my own high standards.

The phone trilled and startled me. Who could this be? Surely not...?

"Hello?" I said nervously.

"Hello, Anna. You sound strained, Are you alright?" Not waiting for me to answer, he went on. "I'm on my way home."

I mumbled something in reply, but he didn't seem to notice, and I went back downstairs.

"Oh no!" I groaned as I looked around the kitchen. Richard would be home in half an hour and I hadn't even finished the pastry for the pie. I pulled out the vegetable basket and placed the cauliflower and carrots on a chopping board. This was ridiculous. I get a five minute phone call and I spend the rest of the afternoon worrying about dead bodies.

"I really don't think I can go through with it." I said to the cauliflower I was dissecting.

Knowing there was only one thing to do, I dried my hands on the kitchen towel, took a deep breath, and picked up the phone.

"Hello?" She started to speak but I ignored her and rushed out my words.

"I know you had to pull some strings for me to go to the morgue for the character research. I'm really sorry but I think someone else should go instead of me—" I ignored her protest. "—and then they can play the dead body in your murder mystery. I'd rather not be the corpse. I'd be much happier with an easier part."

Stanley and Eleanor

My love is made of stone.
I wait until she's all alone
Then I sidle up to her
She doesn't move, or stir
Her voice is never heard
nor that of the tiny bird,
which never leaves her side.
My love has never cried,
lonely on a bench, she
ignores my company.
Known by most the world,
folk pass without a word,
They often stop to stare,
never show they care,
except to take a selfie.
She made four boys wealthy,
with her number one story.
They took all the glory.
With my love I'll lie forever
We will always be together.
No one could know you more
than I do, my sweet Eleanor.

What? She's bronze not stone
You've just ruined my poem.
Nothing rhymes with bronze...

The Eleanor sculpture sits on Stanley Street.

Lost Baby

I often sit and think of you,
of all I dreamed and hoped and planned.
I never got to hold you,
or see your smile, or hold your hand.
But though I cannot see you
I can feel your gentle touch,
you know that we still think of you,
and love you just as much.
I'll never hear you call me mum,
but in peaceful, thoughtful hours,
I hear you in the bird song son,
and see your beauty in the flowers.
And when I'm feeling lonely,
and oft times when I've cried;
I've felt your hug around me,
and sensed you by my side.

For baby Mark born too soon.

When You Came Into My Life

(A wedding reading - *When we were searching
for suitable wedding readings for our daughters
wedding I was inspired to write this*)

It was the start of an ordinary day.
The wind was cold, the sky was grey.
There was nothing to do and nowhere to go.
The day was mundane, the news was slow.

Then you burst into my life.

We had a chat, then talked some more.
The hours flew past, the days a blur...
As we came to the end of each comfortable day,
Goodbye was a word getting harder to say.

Then you moved into my life.

We shared a house, the chores, the food.
We shared the music, friends and mood.
Life together was chugging along.
Everything right, nothing was wrong.

When you came into my life.

We shared our days, our months, the years.
We shared the joys, and soothed the tears.
There wasn't a boundary our love was beyond.
And there wasn't a person who didn't respond,

When you asked to share my life.

Everyone's faces shone with delight.
Our present was happy, our future is bright.
I will vow to love you through thin and through

thick.
Even pose and smile to the cameras...Click!

When we become man and wife.

The End

About the Author

Formerly a textile artist and design consultant for a craft company, Awen Thornber produced craft projects and articles for magazines, and had a regular craft column in Northern Life magazine. She is always looking for inspiration to spark her creative mind and currently devotes her time to writing novels.

Born and bred in Lancashire, Awen also loves walking, painting, ballroom and ballet dancing.

80215362R00074

Made in the USA
Columbia, SC
14 November 2017